Three, Three, The Rivals

ANTHEA FRASER

Three, Three, The Rivals

St. Martin's Press
New York

"A Thomas Dunne Book"

ISBN 0-312-11902-X

First published in Great Britain by HarperCollins Publishers

First U.S. Edition: March 1995
10 9 8 7 6 5 4 3 2 1

To Fiona and Forrest, with love.

GREEN GROW THE RUSHES-O

I'll sing you one-O!
(*Chorus*) Green grow the rushes-O!
     What is your one-O?
One is one and all alone and evermore shall be so.

I'll sing you two-O!
(*Chorus*) Green grow the rushes-O!
     What are your two-O?
Two, two, the lily-white Boys, clothed all in green-O,
(*Chorus*) One is one and all alone and evermore shall be so.

I'll sing you three-O!
(*Chorus*) Green grow the rushes-O!
     What are your three-O?
Three, three, the Rivals,
(*Chorus*) Two, two, the lily-white Boys,
  clothed all in green-O,
One is one and all alone and evermore shall be so.

Four for the Gospel-makers.
Five for the Symbols at your door.
Six for the six proud Walkers.
Seven for the seven Stars in the sky.
Eight for the April Rainers.
Nine for the nine bright Shiners.
Ten for the ten Commandments.
Eleven for the Eleven that went up to Heaven.
Twelve for the twelve Apostles.

Three, Three, The Rivals

CHAPTER 1

She woke suddenly, the scream which had echoed through her dream a strangled gargle in her throat. For a moment she lay unmoving, eyes stretched open to the darkness, still in the thrall of nightmare. Then, cautiously, she released her breath, easing tense muscles and aware of the sweat coursing over her body. Beside her, untouched by her fear, Colin slept serenely, his breathing deep and regular. With an effort, she forced her own to the same rhythm—in, out, in, out—until the clattering of her heart subsided.

What had brought that on? she wondered shakily. It was thirty years since she'd experienced the night-terrors which had plagued her childhood, making every bedtime an endurance test. Humbling, too, that in adulthood the dream still had the power to devastate her.

It would have been their conversation over tea, she thought as her head cleared. Though she'd firmly pushed it out of mind, it must have lodged in her subconscious and resurrected old fears.

She levered herself on to one elbow and peered at the clock. Three-fifteen; an appropriate time for nightmares to ride, but four hours before she was due to wake. Yet she daren't risk sleep again; the dream still lurked in the corners of her mind, ready to pounce as soon as she relaxed.

She'd make a cup of tea; the familiarity of the kitchen would restore her balance. Despite the summer night, she shivered as she fumbled for her dressing-gown, located it and wrapped it tightly about her. Then, feeling her way, she moved towards the door.

Once on the landing she switched the light on, and the everydayness of her surroundings was an immediate palliative. Stephen's jacket over the banister and his closed bedroom door confirmed he was safely home despite the dreaded motorbike.

She started down the stairs, walking at the edge of the treads to avoid the squeaks in the wood. At the window on the half-landing she paused as she always did to look down at the Garden Centre. Though its windows mirrored the lights of the main road, deep shadows surrounded it and, still reluctant to peer into shadows, she continued her descent. The grandfather clock ticked placidly in the hall and a remembrance of last night's supper lingered in the air.

She pushed open the kitchen door and, as the room flooded with light, Jason the labrador looked up from his basket and sleepily thudded his tail. The cat, as always stretched out on the boiler, opened one eye and closed it again. Sheila filled the kettle and plugged it in.

Ridiculous, at her age, to be so thrown by a bad dream. In mitigation, though, it wasn't just any dream, but the one that had haunted her all those years ago. God forbid she was in for another cycle.

Waiting for the kettle to boil, she leaned against the work-surface and looked contentedly about her, grateful for the restoration of normality. Still basically a farm kitchen, the room was warm and welcoming, scented by the dried herbs which hung in clusters from the beams. They'd inherited the large, scrubbed table with the house and sometimes, standing at it to knead bread or prepare her jams and pickles, Sheila wondered about the other women who had used it over the years.

She poured boiling water into the pot and, unhooking a mug, went to sit at the table. The cat abandoned the boiler and jumped on her knee, settling down with a contented purr. Sheila stroked him absent-mindedly, her thoughts still on her unwise disclosure.

Stupid to have let herself be drawn like that; she should simply have let it go. But Angela's dogmatic attitude annoyed her, and she'd spoken without thinking.

What had started them on ghosts, anyway? It was an unusual topic for three down-to-earth countrywomen, whose conversation was more likely to revolve round the price of fertilizer and the long-range weather forecast. Then she remembered: it was the film Janet had seen. 'Honestly,' she'd finished laughingly, after describing its eerie goings-on, 'when it came to bedtime, I was afraid to put the light out!'

Which was when Angela started pontificating. 'Really, Janet, I thought you'd more sense,' she said in her committee voice. 'Ghosts, indeed! How can you be frightened of something that doesn't exist?'

And Sheila, irritated by such bland assurance, had broken almost a lifetime's silence before she realized what was happening. 'Oh, they exist all right,' she heard herself say. 'I've seen one.'

Immediately the words were out she'd have paid any price to retract them, but it was too late. Her friends were staring at her in disbelief. Sheila Fairchild, most level-headed and dependable of women, had seen a *ghost*?

Angela, naturally, was the first to find her voice. 'You're not serious?'

Instantly recanting, Sheila smiled and shook her head. 'Not really.' If only they'd accept that!

But Janet was not to be sidetracked. 'You sounded serious to me. Come on, Sheila—out with it! You saw a ghost? When? Who?'

'Oh, it was forty-odd years ago. I probably imagined it.' But she knew she had not. And of course they would not be satisfied till she'd gone through the whole thing—the forbidden excursion after dark, the quiet graveyard, the terrifying figure.

It was a curious experience, talking about it after all these years. And the unreality was compounded when, coming to an end, she looked up to see Mr Makepeace at the next table, staring at her. The realization that he must have heard every word caused her cheeks to burn. He made her uncomfortable at the best of times, due to the family feud which had started before she was born. Now, he'd heard her make a complete fool of herself. No wonder he was staring.

She had gathered her things together and made a hasty departure, as much to escape his gaze as her friends' continuing questions. But that hadn't been the end of it. Unbelievably, he had phoned last evening while she was out. Mr Makepeace! She'd never spoken to him in her life.

'Sheila! What the hell are you doing?'

She jumped, looking up to see her husband in the doorway, hair ruffled and eyes blinking in the bright light. 'Do you know what time it is?'

'Getting on for four, I suppose. I'm sorry; did I wake you?'

'No, I just turned over and you weren't there. What are you *doing?*'

'I—couldn't sleep.' She had never told Colin of her dream, and it seemed pointless to do so now.

'Anything on your mind?'

'Not particularly.'

'You do too much, you know. I'm always telling you. Meetings and committees and Lord knows what, on top of a full day's work here. No wonder your brain's over-active.' He came into the room, selected a mug and joined her at the table.

'It doesn't usually affect me.' She watched him as he sipped his tea. He'd changed surprisingly little in the twenty years of their marriage. The shock of curly hair was only faintly tinged with grey and he still looked like an overgrown schoolboy, an impression enhanced by the outdoor life he'd chosen against the wishes of his father. His clear, healthily tanned skin was almost free of the stress lines apparent on other men his age.

He met her assessing eyes over the rim of his mug, unperturbed by their scrutiny. 'Did you see Lyn's note about Makepeace phoning?'

'Yes, isn't it amazing? Whatever could he have wanted?'

'To bury the hatchet, perhaps. Now your father and Dick Vernon are both gone, it's all pretty pointless.'

'But why wait this long?' Sheila objected. 'Dad's been dead four years.'

'Will you ring him back?'

'Probably, out of curiosity. I'll get the details from Lyn in the morning.'

Colin stifled a yawn and she stood up, tipping the indignant cat to the floor. 'Come on, you need your sleep. I'll come back up with you.'

It would be all right now, she thought as she preceded Colin up the stairs. The break had dispelled her attack of the vapours and she wouldn't let it happen again. As for the story she told her friends, she'd try to persuade them it had been a joke.

In fact, the disquieting aura of the dream was not so easily dismissed, possibly because it was rooted in reality. It lingered on throughout the morning, leaving Sheila faintly uneasy and tainting the bright summer day with its menace.

Nor could she get Mr Makepeace out of her mind, wishing uselessly that she'd been in to take his call; Lyn said he'd refused to leave a message. She was tempted to phone him, but the peculiar circumstances of their acquaintance deterred her. Better wait for him to ring back.

Determinedly pushing such distractions aside, she turned to the routine matters of her day. Breakfast had been eaten in its customary silence, Lyn had caught the bus to college, Colin and Stephen were at the Garden Centre. Glancing out of the window, she saw that one or two cars were already turning into its gateway. Upstairs, the sound of the vacuum cleaner confirmed that Betty Marsworth was at work.

Satisfied, Sheila walked through to the office which adjoined the kitchen and, leaning over the desk, studied her diary. The day's programme was as always neatly set out, and she skimmed through it to check that nothing had been overlooked. It was of supreme importance to her that she should be organized and efficient, in control of herself and her affairs.

This morning there were the week's standing orders to see to. She must also remember to slip out to the greenhouse and check the stock of dieffenbachia; there'd been a run on them yesterday and a delivery wasn't due till next week. This afternoon, since it was the beginning of the month, would be given over to the accounts, and she was guest speaker at a local meeting this evening. She made a quick note to look over her speech.

There was also a list of phone-calls to make, but after a moment's thought she decided to leave those until later and keep the line clear for Mr Makepeace.

However, as the morning progressed and she dealt systematically with her workload, the phone remained stubbornly silent. Perhaps he'd changed his mind. Sheila promised herself that if she hadn't heard from him by supper-time, she'd take the initiative and call him herself. Almost as she reached the decision, the phone at last rang, and, her mouth suddenly dry, she reached for it. 'The Old Farmhouse.'

But the voice that answered her was Janet's. 'Sheila, have you heard? About Billy Makepeace?'

She frowned, confused to hear the name she'd expected in a different context. 'What about him?'

'He was found in the canal this morning.'

'The canal?' she repeated blankly.

'Yes, drowned. He started to walk home along the towpath, and they think he lost his footing and fell in.'

'You mean he's *dead?*'

'Of course he's dead; he must have been in the water all night, poor old chap. And to think he was in the café as large as life only yesterday.'

'But that's—awful.' Sheila thought of the old man as she'd last seen him, his large frame balanced precariously on the spindly chair, his eyes intent on her face. Now she'd never know why he phoned.

'It seems worse, somehow, when we saw him so recently.' Janet gave a nervous laugh. 'He certainly seemed riveted by your ghost story!'

'I hope he didn't believe it,' Sheila said, even at this point conscious of the need to retract.

'Don't tell me you were pulling our leg?' Janet sounded both indignant and disappointed.

'Oh, come on, Janet! What do you think?'

'It sounded pretty convincing to me.'

'It was meant to; Angela was being so superior, I decided to take her down a peg.'

'Well, you certainly fooled me. And old Billy too, judging by his expression. He was probably looking over his shoulder for ghosties when he lost his footing.'

'Nonsense!' Sheila said sharply. 'He'd never have been taken in by such drivel, and I'm surprised you were.' Uncomfortably aware that she sounded like Angela, she added more quietly, 'What was he doing in La Brioche, anyway? It's hardly his scene.'

'Waiting for his daughter; she arrived just after you left. Well, I must make a start on the lunch but I thought you'd like to know, even though your families weren't on speaking terms.'

Until, apparently, the day he died, when he'd tried to contact her.

'Yes, thanks for phoning, Janet. And my apologies about that ghost business.'

The subject of Makepeace's death dominated the conversation over lunch.

'Do you think it really was him who phoned last night?' Stephen asked. 'Perhaps it was a hoax, someone doing it for a bet.'

Sheila frowned. 'Why on earth should it be a hoax?'

'Well, he's never even acknowledged your existence, has he? Why, suddenly, should he phone you?'

'I've no idea.'

'What really happened, Mum, all those years ago?' Stephen helped himself to more pie, totally unaware of his mother's discomfiture. 'There were three of them, weren't there? Grandad and Mr Makepeace and that Mr Vernon, who disappeared?'

She nodded.

'But what started it all?'

'Oh, they'd been rivals since schooldays, taking it in turns to be top of the class.'

'But it must have been more than that,' Stephen objected, 'for them to stop speaking to each other.'

'Not necessarily,' his mother said thoughtfully. 'Sometimes the worst quarrels are over the most trivial things. If the people involved are stubborn, no one'll give way so it's never patched up.'

'But—'

'That'll do, Stephen,' Colin interposed. 'You know it's not a topic we discuss.'

'Not while Gran and Grandad were alive, but—'

'I said that'll do. Now, get on with your meal, will you? We've a delivery at two.'

It wasn't until DCI Webb reached his flat that evening that he glanced at the paper he'd bought on the way home. But as he dropped it on the kitchen table his eye fell on the photograph displayed on the front page and, registering the headline, he gave an exclamation. LOCAL LANDOWNER DIES, he read, his eyes racing down the paragraph.

The body of Mr William Makepeace, 78, of Longacre Farm, Erlesborough, was recovered from the Avon & Broadshire Canal this morning, after his wife had reported him missing.

Mr Makepeace had spent the evening at the Farmers' Club and had set off as usual to walk home along the towpath. An inquest will be held tomorrow morning.

Born at Longacre Farm, where he still lived . . .

Webb turned abruptly from the table and poured himself a drink. Quite suddenly he had need of it. After a couple of almost medicinal sips he returned, glass in hand, to the story. So old Billy was dead. Reading between the lines, he'd probably had one too many, and the towpath was narrow for an unsteady gait.

He stood for several minutes staring at the strong, fleshy face in the photograph, wishing the canal had not been involved in the death; it had been an intrinsic part of his boyhood—a favourite place to fish or paddle or while away long hours watching the activity at the locks. And, as he grew older, to walk with old Makepeace's daughter. Now, his memories of it would be tarnished.

Still, there it was; old Billy, the last of the three, was dead, and a less than edifying chapter finally closed. He stared unseeingly into his glass as memories he had always stifled stirred uneasily.

Thank God he was dining with Hannah this evening, he thought, turning away to refresh his drink; he would not have welcomed his own company. Leaving the paper spread on the table, he carried his glass through to the bathroom and turned on the shower.

'Go easy on the hard stuff, love,' he said an hour later, as Hannah moved to the drinks table. 'I'm a couple ahead of you this evening.'

'Really? Any particular reason?'

'I've had a forced march down memory lane, which I could have done without.'

She handed him his glass, her clear grey eyes on his face. 'What caused that?'

'Tonight's headline in the *News*. Old boy I used to know found dead.'

'Oh, I'm sorry.'

He nodded, accepting her sympathy but volunteering nothing further. After a moment he looked up, caught her considering gaze, and smiled.

'Sorry to be such poor company. Tell me what you've been doing since I saw you.'

Though their flats were in the same building, the lives they led meant that weeks often passed without their seeing each other, an occurrence which, in the unique circumstances of their relationship, worried neither of them.

'The big news is that Gwen's been offered a year's sabbatical in Canada. I'm green with envy.'

Gwen Rutherford was headmistress of Ashbourne School for Girls, one of the most highly regarded in the county, and Hannah was her deputy.

Webb gave a low whistle. 'And you'll hold the fort while she's away?'

'As acting head, yes. But I'd much rather go to Canada!'

He smiled sympathetically. Hannah's parents had lived in Toronto for the last twenty years, and she seldom saw them. 'Your turn next, perhaps. In the meantime, it'll be quite a responsibility.'

She shrugged. 'The governors will keep an eye on me.'

Webb was silent. One of the school governors, Charles Frobisher, had wanted to marry Hannah a few years back; for all Webb knew, he might still. Perhaps, in Gwen's absence, they'd need to see more of each other.

'When is she going?'

'In September—only two months away. Another woman should have gone this year and Gwen was down for next, but now she's dropped out and they've had to move things forward. You know Gwen, she's flapping round like a mad hen, spraying hairpins and panicking about not getting things sorted out in time. In fact, there's little to see to from the school's point of view. We always work closely together, so there shouldn't be any problems.'

'Her mother lives with her, doesn't she? Is she going too?'

'No, it would be too much for her. She'll spend the year with her other daughter.'

Webb sipped his drink, grateful for the distraction Hannah's news had provided. 'Whereabouts in Canada?'

'The outskirts of Toronto, would you believe?'

'There ain't no justice.'

She put her glass down. 'If you'll excuse me, I'll see to the meal.'

As she left the room, Webb too rose and walked restlessly to the window, looking down on the brown grass and parched earth. Another hot summer was under way and everywhere lay baking under the remorseless sun. Near the house, patches of wet earth on the flowerbeds marked the progress of a conscientious gardener—probably Mrs Taverner from No. 3.

Even as her name came to mind she appeared beneath him, jug in hand, and made her way carefully over the grass to the birdbath. He watched as she filled it with clean water, totally absorbed in her task. Seen from above, she was a strange figure in her floral cotton dress and ancient straw hat, her scrawny legs ending in ankle socks and sandals. In different but equally eccentric gear she performed similar duties in winter, scattering seeds and crusts and ferociously chasing off any cat unwise enough to be lurking near.

Now, even before she'd reached the house, an assortment of starlings fluttered down and began to splash in the shallow basin, squawking and fighting for a share in the treat.

Behind him, Hannah's voice said, 'Dinner's ready,' and he turned to follow her into the dining-room.

Throughout the meal—chilled watercress soup, poached salmon, fresh raspberries—Webb responded to Hannah's queries, volunteered snippets of news, and generally felt he was making a contribution to the evening. But over coffee she startled him by saying, 'You're still brooding over that old man's death, aren't you? Who was he?'

He looked up quickly, but her face was in shadow. The light had almost gone as the last glow of sunset faded from the sky, and the candle on the table illuminated only its polished surface.

'Just an old farmer I knew years ago,' he answered dismissively.

'In Erlesborough?'

He nodded.

She reached for the coffee-pot and refilled his cup. 'David, why do you never speak of the past? I know you have a sister, because you spend Christmas with her, but any time I ask about her, or anything to do with your childhood, you very adroitly change the subject.'

'I'd no idea I was so devious.'

'On the contrary, I'm sure it's quite deliberate.'

He moved restlessly, his fingers playing with the unused cutlery by his plate. 'There's little to tell. It wasn't a particularly happy childhood, and I prefer not to think about it, that's all.'

'But this old man's death has brought it back?'

'Inevitably.'

She laughed, giving a little shrug of defeat. 'All right, you win.'

'It's not particularly interesting,' he said defensively. 'I can't think—'

He was interrupted by the ringing of his mobile phone. 'Excuse me.' He pushed back his chair and went out into the dark hallway where he'd left it.

'DCI Webb.'

The Chief Superintendent's voice sounded in his ear. 'Spider. Sorry to disturb your evening, but we've been landed with a suspicious death. That old chap they pulled out of the canal. Report to me first thing, would you?'

He must have made some reply, because Fleming, satisfied, had rung off and a buzzing came over the line. The flickering candlelight from the open doorway lit a patch of carpet to pale rose and as he stared at it, Hannah's cat walked gracefully across it and disappeared into the shadows beyond.

Webb sighed and put the phone down. It seemed that all his evasive action had been in vain. The past would have to be faced after all.

CHAPTER 2

They drove out to Erlesborough in silence. Sergeant Jackson, after one look at the Governor's set face, decided it was best to hold his peace. He could have sworn he knew all Spiderman's moods, but he was out of his depth on this one. All right, the Guv knew the victim, but so what? It wasn't the first time it had happened—something of an occupational hazard—and anyway he didn't seem to have seen him in years. So what was he so uptight about? With a mental shrug, Jackson settled down to his driving.

Erlesborough lay due west of Shillingham, some fifteen miles along the Oxbury road. It was a pleasant little market town, mainly Georgian in architecture but with roots going back to Roman times and beyond. A Benedictine abbey had once occupied the site and its ruins still stood in the gardens behind the High Street, a haven of peace and greenery only steps from the bustling market-place. Jackson knew it well from runs out with Millie and the children; knew, too, the canal to the south of the town, which figured in the present case.

The fields and woodlands through which they had been driving fell away behind them as they entered the outskirts of the town. To the left of the road stood the buildings and playing fields of St Anne's School, traditional rivals of Shillingham's Ashbourne. Then the road curved round past a large supermarket, new since Jackson's last visit, and into the wide High Street where, on this Wednesday morning, the market was in full swing.

Jackson slowed down perforce, inching forward behind a string of cars, and beside him Webb stirred restlessly.

'Silver Street first, Guv?' Which was the address of the police station.

Webb grunted, which Jackson took to be assent. He turned left, thankfully leaving the mêlée of the High Street, and drove into the cobbled street which ended, some two hundred yards ahead, in a cul-de-sac. As he slowed down outside the tall, narrow building occupied by Broadshire Constabulary, Webb said abruptly, 'There's a car park behind, along the alleyway there.'

Moments later they were walking back down the alley to the front entrance of the police station, the sunshine warm on their heads and shoulders. The duty sergeant looked up as they pushed their way through the swing-doors.

'DCI Webb and Sergeant Jackson to see DI Charlton. We're expected.'

'Yes, sir. One moment.' He spoke into a telephone, and then, releasing the security door, signalled a young constable to take the visitors upstairs.

Detective-Inspector Charlton, a large, heavy-set man, rose to his feet and came round his desk to greet them. 'Good morning, sir, Sergeant. Sorry to drag you over here, but as you'll have heard, our DCI's away on a course and this has turned into a major inquiry.'

Webb nodded and introduced Jackson. 'So, what have we got?'

'Well, to be honest, the PM findings were a shock. We never doubted it was anything but an accident. After all, Mr Makepeace was a well-known and respected figure in the town.'

'Not the sort to get himself murdered?' asked Webb drily.

The other man flushed. 'You know what I mean, sir.'

'The full report isn't through, of course, but I gather there were unexplained pressure marks at the base of the skull.'

'That's correct. It's believed his head was forcibly held under water.'

'A fair bit of pressure would have been needed; he was a heavy man.'

'Unless he was inhibited by the cold water, sir. And he'd been drinking, mind.'

'No sign of a coronary?'

'No, and that's surprising, too. Had a bit of trouble with his ticker over the last year or two, did Mr Makepeace.'

'Who found him?'

'Mr Martin Allerdyce, sir. He's a partner in Henshaw and Allerdyce, solicitors in the High Street. Lives out on the Oxbury road and walks to work along the towpath every morning. Here's his statement.'

Charlton pushed some papers across the desk and Webb ran his eye rapidly over them. The body had been floating face down against the bank, just along from the railway bridge. Without looking up, he said, 'You've seen his wife?'

'Not since the PM. We heard you were coming and thought you'd want to see her yourself. She was shocked enough yesterday, poor soul, when it seemed accidental. We kept it as brief as possible.' He paused, and when Webb didn't comment, added, 'The men are waiting for your orders, sir. As you'll know, some of your own men have reported in, too.'

'Yes; we can't commandeer all your personnel, but we'll need some for local knowledge. What about the scene?'

'It's still roped off, but the SOCOs have finished now.'

'Right, thanks, Inspector. We'll get on with the briefing, then.'

The Inspector led the way along the linoleumed corridor and pushed open a door at the far end. Jackson followed the two men, his unease growing. He'd worked closely with the DCI over a number of years, and today's attitude was unprecedented; it was as though he were having to force himself to act in the manner expected of him.

The briefing did nothing to reassure Jackson, and glances he intercepted between the Shillingham men showed that they, too, were aware of undercurrents. His own overriding impression was that for some reason he couldn't fathom, the Governor did not want to handle the case.

The facts as known were gone over, action teams set up and the next briefing arranged for five o'clock. Jackson sat throughout in unaccustomed gloom, paying attention but, affected by Webb's attitude, not feeling part of the team.

As the meeting finished and the men dispersed, Webb beckoned him over. 'Ken, it's now eleven-thirty. I'd like you to go along to the solicitors and have a word with Mr Allerdyce. I imagine he's clean, but we know how often murderers "find" bodies. The DI knows and respects the man; I need an unbiased opinion. After that, you might look in at the Farmers' Club—it's sure to be open on market day. Speak to the barman and get the names of those who were drinking with Makepeace, those who left at the same time—the usual guff. I have a few things to do so I'll take the car and meet you at the Narrow Boat in an hour's time.'

Webb came out of the swing-doors and turned towards the alleyway leading to the car park. Then, obeying an impulse, he passed the turning and walked on to the bottom of the street, which ended in a shoulder-high stone wall. He used to come here after school with a crowd of other small boys; they'd sit on the wall eating chips and watching the movement of the barges on the canal below. At least outwardly, little seemed to have changed.

Resting his arms on the wall, he looked down the grassy bank to the water, serene and blue in the summer sunshine, and, beyond it, to the backs of houses giving on to Lower Road. One of them had been his childhood home, its attendant nursery garden spreading almost to the canal banks. But the rich soil which, during school holidays, he had helped his father to hoe, had long since been grassed over and was as dry and thirsty-looking as its neighbours. For a long moment he stared at it, unwelcome memories stirring. Then he forced his gaze back to the canal.

A couple of barges were moored beneath him, no doubt awaiting police permission to proceed. It would soon be granted; frogmen had already searched the bottom of the canal but found nothing relevant. Glancing to his right, he could see the Narrow Boat public house where he'd arranged to meet Jackson and, beyond it, the Bridge Street allotments.

But he was wasting time; there were things to be done and the sooner he made a start on them, the better. Turning away, he went to retrieve the car. Memories continued to buffet him as he winkled his way back into the traffic on the High Street and made his crawling progress past the Sandon Arms and the Town Hall. Then, reaching the end of the High Street, he joined the faster-moving traffic on the Oxbury road and it was only minutes before he was turning into the familiar gateway of The Old Farmhouse.

He parked the car and stood for a moment looking over

the hedge at the Garden Centre. It seemed quite busy for a week day; people were hurrying in all directions with long flat trolleys loaded with plants, and several cars were waiting their turn to go through the gates.

But he hadn't come here to stand and watch them. He walked purposefully to the house and rang the bell. Somewhere inside the dog barked. Then there was the sound of footsteps and his sister opened the door.

'David!'

'Hello, Sheila.'

Though they hadn't seen each other since Christmas, they did not embrace. They'd never been a demonstrative family.

'Come in. I was half-expecting you.'

He patted the dog which had come to greet him and followed her through to the kitchen, which smelt of baking.

'This is a bit of a bombshell, isn't it?'

'It certainly is. Sit down. Can I get you a coffee?'

'If it's no trouble.'

'None at all.'

She bustled about, setting out cups, putting some newly made gingerbread on a plate.

'How did you hear of it?' he asked her.

'Janet Conway phoned, though at that stage we thought it was an accident. It was only this morning I heard—'

She broke off, turned back to attend to the coffee. He watched her frowningly; she seemed more upset than he'd expected.

'I suppose it *is* true,' she added, setting coffee and gingerbread in front of him, 'about it not being?'

'Afraid so. Had he any enemies, would you say?'

She gave a short, bitter laugh. 'Now Dad's dead, you mean? Well, you can hardly count Dick Vernon; it's donkeys' years since he vanished.' She sipped her coffee. 'It's a sobering thought that of the three of them, Dad was the only one to die naturally.'

'We don't know how—or if—Dick died.'

She looked up at that. 'You surely don't think he'd anything to do with this?'

'No, I don't,' Webb said roundly. 'Though stranger things have happened. I'll have to see old Mrs Vernon, anyway. She's still alive, I take it?'

She nodded absently, and he laid a hand on her arm. 'Sheila, what's the matter? Something's worrying you; is it to do with old Makepeace's death?'

'I'm sorry he's dead, of course, and in such a horrible way. But it's not only that.' She looked up, coming to a decision. Colin was sure to mention it anyway. 'David— something rather odd happened.'

'What?'

'He phoned me. On Monday evening, when I was at WI.'

He stared at her. '*Billy Makepeace?*'

'Yes. I wish to heaven I knew what he wanted.'

'But I don't understand. Were you on speaking terms?'

She shook her head. 'I've never spoken to him in my life —that's what makes it so strange. But that afternoon I'd had tea at a café in the High Street, and he was at the next table.'

'What's that got to do with anything?'

'Nothing, really. Perhaps he—just thought it was time to bury the hatchet.' That had been Colin's suggestion.

'He'd hardly end a lifetime's feud with a phone-call.'

'He might have suggested meeting or something.'

'Well, it seems we'll never know. Who took the message?'

'Lyn.'

Webb grunted. His opinion of his niece was ambivalent. Though she apparently had brains enough to get into college, it was not apparent from her appearance. Small and waif-like, with enormous eyes and straggly hair, she habitually wore clothes too big for her—sloppy sweaters that hung round her hips, sleeves reaching to her fingertips, and dull black skirts flapping round her ankles. To Webb's jaundiced eye she looked more like an appeal for the homeless than the child of relatively affluent parents studying for a degree.

'What exactly did he say?'

'Just asked to speak to me. Lyn said I was out, and he seemed a bit deflated, she thought. She asked if there was any message, but he said it didn't matter and hung up. If I'd got home at the usual time I'd have phoned back, but there'd been a series of delays and it was after eleven-thirty.'

'What time did he phone?'

'I don't know; I went out at seven-thirty, so after that. Does it matter?'

'I wondered if he'd gone straight to the Farmers' Club after making the phone-call.'

'Again, does it matter?'

'Sheila, at this stage I've no idea what "matters" and what doesn't. I'm just trying to fill in his last few hours. You say he was in the café that day; was he alone?'

'While I was there, but Janet said his daughter joined him later.' Sheila looked at him with a half-smile. 'Didn't you once carry a torch for Jenny Makepeace?'

'There's been a lot of water under the bridge since then.'

'She married Jim Hawthorn but it didn't work out. She's now head receptionist at the Sandon Arms.'

'Any children?'

'No.'

'What about the old couple: did they go out much?'

'Billy did; he was quite a big noise, you know. A magistrate, for one thing, and on the town council. I saw him around quite a lot, specially on market days. Not Mrs Makepeace, though; she's partially blind and doesn't get about much these days. There's been a farm manager at Longacre since Billy developed his heart trouble, though from all accounts he still kept a very close eye on things.'

'Do you know him—the manager?'

'Only by sight.' She added ironically, 'He's part of the enemy camp, so there's no contact between us.'

'Or the Vernons?'

'Or the Vernons.'

'Well, there'll be some contact now. With me, at any rate. And with the three men gone, it's more than time the whole nonsense was forgotten. What's the manager's name?'

'Croft, Jerry Croft. He looks pleasant enough, and his wife too. She's a schoolteacher—takes the entry class at St Gay's.'

St Gay's! The once-familiar abbreviation leapt at him out of the past, blessedly unsullied by modern usage. His happiest childhood memories were of St Gabriel's Church School at the top of the High Street.

He wrenched his mind back to the present. 'Would you say he had any reason to shove his boss into the canal?'

Sheila shuddered. 'How awful it must be, having to suspect everyone.'

Webb pushed back his chair and walked to the window, looking down the long garden which sloped towards the canal. 'It seems Billy made a habit of walking home along the towpath. At what point would he come up on to the main road?'

'Directly opposite the farm. There are open fields facing Longacre, so there's easy access to and from the towpath.'

'You've access yourself?'

'Yes, there's a gate in the bottom fence.'

'Do you often go down there?'

'Sometimes. It makes a pleasant stroll.'

'Ever come face to face with old Billy?'

'Never. But I think he only used it to go to and from the club. He went everywhere else in his Land-Rover.'

Webb glanced at his watch. 'I'd better be on my way. Thanks for the coffee, Sheila, and the information. If you think of anything else, will you let me know?'

'Yes, of course.' She hesitated. 'When you see Mrs Makepeace, pass on our condolences, will you? And say if there's anything I can do, to let me know.'

He smiled at her. 'Thanks, I will.'

'Are you going straight over there?'

'No, I'm meeting up with my sergeant now. And there are various people I want to speak to before I see the Makepeaces.'

'Perhaps his wife will know why he phoned.'

'You may be sure I'll ask her.'

She stood in the doorway as he walked over the gravel to the car. Then, as he bent to get into it, she called after him. 'David, if you need to stay overnight at all, you're welcome to come here.'

'Thanks, I'll bear that in mind.'

The inside of the car was unbearably hot and he wound down all the windows. Over the hedge the Garden Centre was still doing thriving business. Lifting his hand in farewell, Webb eased his way out on to the main road and turned back towards Erlesborough.

The Narrow Boat pub was a popular lunch-time venue, particularly, in the summer, the tables outside overlooking the canal. Webb saw Jackson ensconced at one as he came out of the bar door, and walked over the grass to join him. He was aware that he'd been short with Ken and owed him an explanation. The trouble was knowing where to start.

'Got you a pint lined up, Guv, since there was such a crush at the bar. I've kept it cool in the shade.'

'Thanks.' Webb took a deep, appreciative draught. 'How did you get on?'

'The solicitor seems OK, but it turns out Makepeace was one of their clients.'

'Ah-ha! Then he'll need a closer look than if he'd fished a complete stranger out of the water. Mind, in a town this size most people are connected in one way or another.'

'He seemed quite shaken, specially now it's a murder case.'

'Had he any ideas on possible suspects?'

Jackson studiously avoided his eye. 'Not really.'

'Go on, Ken. What did he say?'

'That the only one he could think of was dead himself.' Jackson's eyes were still on his plate.

'Did he give a name?'

The sergeant flushed, but answered doggedly, 'John Webb, Guv.'

'Who, you will doubtless have deduced, was my father.'

'It did seem a coincidence, like. Specially since—' He broke off and hastily drained his tankard.

'Specially since I've been behaving like a bear with a sore head ever since this case came up? I'm sorry, Ken. I was going to put you in the picture, even before this. Get yourself a refill and while you're at it, grab us a couple of pies, and then I'll fill you in.'

Jackson was quite a while—the bar was busy and he had to wait his turn for the food—but Webb scarcely noticed his absence. He sat morosely staring down at the table, where the shadow of the umbrella moved lazily in the faint breeze and forgotten images flickered in front of his eyes: fights in the school playground; his father's face, tight with anger; a girl in a cotton dress. They belonged in the past, he told himself, they had no power over him now. But he knew their shadow lay heavily across him.

'It's like a madhouse in there.' Jackson stood above him, offloading glasses and plates from a round tin tray, and the cheerful clatter broke the spell.

Webb roused himself and helped to distribute the cutlery. 'Right, Ken,' he said, as Jackson seated himself, 'while we eat I'll sketch in some of the background.' He cut a piece of pie, loaded it with mustard and pickle, then laid his knife down again. Jackson, however, curious though he was to know the Governor's rôle in all this, did not allow the fact to stay his appetite, and tucked in with enthusiasm.

Webb watched him in silence for a few minutes, clenching the handle of his tankard. Then he cleared his throat. 'You'll have gathered that I grew up in this town.'

Jackson nodded. 'You'd never mentioned it before, though.' It had come as a surprise to him, while he waited at the bar, to realize how little he knew of Webb's background.

Webb continued as if he hadn't spoken. 'Consequently I knew Makepeace when I was a boy, though I wasn't allowed to speak to him.'

Jackson looked up at that and Webb nodded heavily. 'I

know it sounds absurd but he, my father and another man were sworn enemies and all us children were supposed to carry on the feud.'

'Sounds like the Mafia,' commented Jackson with his mouth full.

'They took it just about as seriously, as I discovered when I broke the rule and got beaten for it.'

Jackson had a wild, disturbing image of himself taking the strap to Paul or Tim, and dismissed it as untenable. 'That was a bit steep,' he said.

'It was my own fault. My father was a hard man, and his word was law.'

'But what caused the upset in the first place?'

'It went back to their schooldays, though I don't know the details. It was never talked about in my presence and surreptitious questions got me nowhere.'

Jackson ate for some minutes in silence. Then he asked, 'What about the other chap? You said there were three of them.'

'That was odd—one of those unexplained disappearances. One evening he told his wife he was going out for cigarettes and was never seen again.'

'Good grief! How long ago was that?'

Webb shrugged. 'Forty years or so.'

'And they never found out what happened to him?'

'Nope. But he was in an emotional state at the time and it was assumed he'd lost his memory. He could still be alive somewhere, leading a seemingly normal life but with no knowledge of his past.'

Jackson shook his head wonderingly, grateful for his own uneventful childhood.

'None of this is particularly relevant,' Webb went on more briskly, 'but since you might hear some wild stories during this investigation, I thought it as well to put the facts straight. And you've my permission to pass them on to the lads should the need arise.'

Jackson pushed his empty plate away and said thoughtfully, 'Will they speak to you now, Guv? The families, I mean.'

'They won't have much option. I'm the investigating officer in a murder case.'

'But it might make things awkward, like.'

'The Chief Super doesn't think so,' Webb said drily. 'Naturally I told him the position, but he felt the background knowledge would be useful.' He thought briefly of Fleming's airy dismissal of his doubts. 'Anyway, Ken, how did you get on at the Farmers' Club?' And at last he picked up his knife and fork and began to eat.

'They were all discussing it when I arrived. Only too ready to answer questions, including several I didn't ask, but nothing really useful came up. As we know, Makepeace had been in on Monday night. He arrived late, which was unusual, and seemed to have something on his mind. Didn't join in as he normally did.'

'Was any reason given?'

'No; several of them asked if he was all right, but he just brushed them off.'

'Did he leave at the normal time?'

'Yes, soon after eleven. A couple of other men left with him and they walked along Bridge Street together as far as the bridge, where Makepeace went down the steps to the towpath.'

'They didn't see anyone else down there?'

'No.'

'Well, it wasn't a mugging; there was over a hundred pounds in his wallet. So who did he meet on the towpath, Ken? And was the meeting a chance one, or carefully planned?'

'We need to go back through the day, don't we, Guv? There might be a lead there.'

'Well, for a start we know he was at a café in the High Street about four o'clock.'

Jackson looked surprised. 'Do we?'

'So my sister tells me.'

This time, Jackson bit back his surprise. Strewth, the

Governor was playing this one close to his chest, for all his apparent openness. So that was where he'd been before lunch.

'What I'd like to know,' Webb was continuing, 'is why he was late arriving at the club. He'd have been on foot, of course. But first—' he pushed the remaining food to the side of his plate—'we'd better have a word with the police surgeon. What was his name again?'

'Dr Adams,' Jackson said.

'Good lord—really? I didn't pick that up at the briefing.' Which didn't surprise Jackson—the Governor hadn't been his usual astute self by any means. 'Fancy him still being around,' he was continuing. 'He came here when he was newly qualified and married old Nairn's receptionist a year or two later.'

Jackson supposed stoically that the Chief Super knew what he was doing, but this remembrance-of-times-past routine was getting a bit much, and the case had only just started.

'Right, Ken, we'll start with Dr Adams and see where that gets us.' And before Jackson had got to his feet, Webb was already striding across the grass towards the pub car park.

CHAPTER 3

'David was here,' Sheila greeted her husband, when he came in for lunch.

'So it's landed on his plate. There's irony for you. Was it a social call?'

'Not really, he wanted anything I could tell him on Mr Makepeace.'

'You mentioned the phone-call?'

'Yes.'

'What did he make of it?'

'He was as astonished as we were.'

Colin said thoughtfuly, 'It's certainly odd, that the old

man should break the habit of a lifetime on the day he
died.'

Sheila shuddered. 'And after seeing him in the café, too.
In one day, I had more contact with him than I'd had in
my entire life.'

'I'd hardly call being in the same café and a missed phone
call, contact.'

'You know what I mean. Is Stephen coming?'

'In a couple of minutes; he's overseeing a delivery.'

Sheila put the salad bowl on the table. 'It's the first time
I've seen David on duty, but he was just the same. It sounds
silly, but I always think of him more as a policeman than
a brother.'

Colin smiled. 'He is rather a solemn chap. I don't even
remember you being close as children.'

'No, he was very much the elder brother. And it didn't
help that Dad always spoiled me and was hard on him,
probably because he was the boy.'

The back door was flung open and Stephen came in,
putting an end to the discussion. Abandoning her reminiscences, his mother started to serve the lunch.

The doctor's house was where it had always been, halfway
up the hill which led off the High Street. Webb's gratifi-
cation at finding it was, however, tempered on reading the
neatly framed notice on the gate.

SURGERY HOURS

Doctors Adams, Sinclair and Barnes hold their surgery at the Health Centre, 124 Bridge Street, from
9.0 a.m.–11.0 a.m. and from 5.0 p.m.–7.0 p.m. every
weekday. In case of emergency, telephone Erlesborough 7653.

Webb swore softly and glanced at his watch. It was just
after two. 'We might catch him in his lunch-hour,' he said
over his shoulder to Jackson, and walked up the gravelled

path to the door. A pale woman in late middle-age answered his ring, in whom Webb could just recognize the pretty receptionist of forty years ago.

'I'm sorry, the surgery—' she began, but Webb cut her short.

'Mrs Adams? I'm Chief Inspector Webb of Shillingham CID. Is the doctor at home?'

Her face cleared. 'Is it concerning Mr Makepeace?'

'That's right.'

The hall was square and carpeted in Turkey red. Against one wall an old-fashioned stand was submerged beneath a mound of raincoats and scarves, and a businesslike black bag lay propped at its feet. They were ushered into the erstwhile waiting-room, long since reclaimed and turned into a pleasant study.

'The doctor won't be a moment.'

Jackson extracted his notebook from his attaché case while Webb, too restless to settle, walked over to the bookshelves and ran his eye along the spines. His name had elicited no response from Mrs Adams; he wondered if her husband had a better memory.

Behind him he heard the door open, and turned quickly. His memory of Frank Adams was of a small, dapper man with dark hair and a neat moustache, who always wore a flower in his lapel. At first glance the little doctor seemed uncannily unchanged—even to the buttonhole. However, a closer look revealed that although he still had a moustache and a full head of hair, both were now steel-grey.

He was advancing towards Webb, holding out his hand. 'Chief Inspector—Webb?' He smiled, losing his uncertainty. 'Davy Webb? It is, isn't it? Well, well! I heard you'd done well for yourself in the police force.'

'Good afternoon, Doctor. It's good to see you again, even in these circumstances. May I introduce my colleague, Sergeant Jackson?'

The doctor shook Jackson's hand equally warmly. 'I was about to have my after-lunch coffee. Can I offer you a cup?'

'That would be kind.'

'I'll ask Vera—ah, here she is. You remember Vera, I suppose?'

'Yes, of course.' Webb smiled at the woman who, anticipating her husband's request, had appeared with a tray.

'I'm sorry,' she murmured, 'I hadn't connected the name. I remember you now.'

The coffee was poured and distributed and Vera Adams left the room, closing the door quietly behind her.

'It's about old Billy, no doubt,' the doctor began, forestalling Webb's opening remark. 'A terrible shock, especially since I now hear it was no accident.'

'You attended the scene, I believe?' After a shaky start the interview had resolved itself into standard procedure, and Webb, back on familiar ground, felt more comfortable.

'That's right. Martin Allerdyce had his mobile phone with him, so no time was lost. He rang Silver Street and then me. PC Stebbins and I arrived within minutes of each other.'

Stebbins had been at the briefing, and his account tallied with the doctor's.

'You'd no reason to doubt that death was accidental?'

'None whatever. I did notice slight bruising, but I supposed he'd acquired it as he fell—there are some thick roots lining the bank thereabouts. In fact, his walking-stick had lodged in them, which reinforced the impression of lost footing. To be honest, if asked for an opinion I'd have gone for coronary thrombosis brought on by shock and the sudden immersion. He had a bypass operation only eighteen months ago.'

'So you assumed he'd tripped, fallen in the water, and had a heart attack before he could haul himself out again?'

'Exactly.'

Webb sipped his coffee thoughtfully. 'Were you aware that Mr Makepeace walked to and from the club along the towpath?'

The doctor smiled ruefully. 'Not only aware of it, Chief Inspector—' Thank God he'd dispensed with 'Davy', Jackson thought—'it was I who instigated it. I felt now he'd given up farm work he wasn't getting enough exercise. He'd hop into that Land-Rover of his rather than walk two hundred yards. Mind you, it wasn't the exercise angle that swung it, but the fact that he could enjoy his drinks without worrying about driving home.'

'The routine was common knowledge, then?'

'I'd say so, among those who knew him.'

'When was the last time you saw him, Doctor?'

'Professionally? About three months ago, when he came in for his last check-up. But we were both sidesmen at St Gabriel's, so we met regularly on that basis.'

'An awkward question now. I imagine you can guess what it is.'

'Can I think of anyone who wanted him dead? The answer is an unqualified "no". Old Billy was stubborn and frequently difficult, and he'd the devil of a temper when roused, but he was regarded as a character and much respected.' The doctor hesitated, then added quietly, 'I appreciate this can't be one of your easiest cases, Mr Webb. However, I'm sure you'll get nothing but cooperation from the family.'

He glanced at Jackson, who politically gazed out of the window. 'I did hope, you know, that things might be patched up before the old men died, but neither would give way.'

Webb nodded and said awkwardly, 'My sister told me how supportive you were during my father's last illness, and my mother's, too. I'm grateful.'

Dr Adams, embarrassed, glanced at the carriage clock above the fireplace. 'Well, if there's nothing else for now, I must get on with my rounds. Needless to say, if I can be of more help, you have only to ask.'

'One last thing: was anything further ever heard of Dick Vernon?'

'Not a word. He simply disappeared off the face of the earth.'

'His wife never heard any more?'

'Not as far as I know. Incredibly, though, it's not all that rare; one reads of similar instances in the press. But you'll know better than I how many people disappear and are never heard of again.'

It had been a necessary but not very productive interview. They were shown out, and the doctor was not long after them. As they sat in the car deliberating on their next move, he came out of the gate and got into the blue Cavalier parked in front of them. Webb watched him drive away.

'Do you reckon this other bloke might have showed up after all these years?' Jackson asked, echoing Sheila's query.

'Not really, no, but there's a remote possibility, and question-marks worry me.'

'You said the men's kids carried on the vendetta: how many were there, apart from you and your sister?'

'Billy Makepeace had a daughter and Dick Vernon twin sons. He was a twin himself.' Webb stirred and sighed. 'Yes, you're right, Ken—I can't put it off any longer. We'll go to Longacre, and while we're there we'll call on the farm manager and see what he has to say.'

For the second time that day Webb found himself driving along the Oxbury road. This time they passed The Old Farmhouse and Garden Centre on their left and continued for another half mile before, on their right, they came to Longacre Farm. As Sheila had said, it looked out over rough land, and there was a trodden-down footpath to one side which presumably led to the canal.

Jackson parked in front of the farm gates and, for the first time in his life, Webb went through them into what even now seemed enemy territory.

The yard was large and clean, with a row of outbuildings straight ahead and the farmhouse to the right. On the left the property was bounded by a beech hedge, in which a gate had been inserted giving access to the adjacent bungalow.

Figuratively gritting his teeth, Webb started towards the house, but before he reached it the door opened and Jenny Hawthorn stood there. Momentarily he paused; then, Jackson at his side, he continued his approach.

The daughter, Jackson surmised, and looked at her with interest. Tall and straight, she held herself proudly, even defensively, which, knowing the circumstances, he couldn't wonder at. But she was a pretty woman, with soft brown hair and large eyes which were fixed on the Governor, clearly waiting for his lead. He gave it smoothly.

'Good afternoon, Mrs Hawthorn. I'm extremely sorry about your father.'

To Jackson's keen eyes she seemed to relax a little. 'Thank you—Chief Inspector, isn't it?'

'That's right.' He introduced Jackson. 'Is it possible to have a word with your mother?'

'She'll see you, of course, but I hope you'll make allowances. She's very distressed and Dr Adams has given her a sedative.'

Webb had to duck his head to enter the house. The building was very old and the ceilings and door-frames low. There was a faint smell, not unpleasant, that Jackson associated with elderly people, but the furniture gleamed and there were fresh flowers on the table.

The old woman was almost lost in the depths of an armchair, her twisted fingers clasped in her lap. Seeing the tinted spectacles, Webb remembered Sheila saying she was losing her sight.

He bent solicitously over her, briefly putting his large hand over both her frail ones. 'Mrs Makepeace, it's David Webb. I'm so very sorry.' He was aware of Jenny's stillness behind him.

The old woman stirred and sighed. 'Yes. Yes, I'm sure you are. It's good of you to come.'

Webb glanced around for a straight-backed chair and, seeing one against the wall, took it over to her side. 'Are you able to answer a few questions? I shan't trouble you with anything that's not important.'

She nodded.

'Did you know your husband rang my sister the evening he died?'

He registered both Jenny's gasp and Jackson's surprise

at a detail he'd neglected to pass on earlier. Mrs Makepeace was leaning forward, peering at him through her clouded eyes. 'Billy rang Sheila Webb?' she said incredulously, and Webb's heart sank. He wouldn't find the answer here.

'He didn't mention it?'

'That he didn't.'

'My niece took the call; Sheila was out, but it would be useful to know why he phoned.'

Mrs Makepeace shook her head decidedly. 'The girl's mistaken. I'm convinced of it.'

'Did he ring *anyone* that evening?'

'Not that I recall.'

Webb turned to Jenny. 'Sheila saw your father in a café that day. I believe you joined him later?'

'That's right, I did.' Her voice was soft and low.

'Which café was it, Mrs Hawthorn?'

'La Brioche. I didn't see your sister, though.'

'Did your father mention she'd been there?'

'No.'

'Did he seem abstracted at all, as though his thoughts were elsewhere?'

She looked surprised. 'Yes, actually, he did. I'd slipped out specially because he was anxious to see my photos of the County Show. But when I produced them, he barely glanced at them.'

'He didn't say what was worrying him?'

'No.'

Webb turned back to the old woman. 'Did your husband lunch at home on Monday, Mrs Makepeace?'

She nodded, her mind still on the mysterious phone-call.

'Was he absent-minded then?'

'Not at all. He was bothered about one of the lambs.'

'Do you know what his plans were that afternoon?'

She thought for a moment. 'He was going to see Jack Rogers about some fencing, then call in at the library. And, of course, he was meeting Jenny here for tea.'

'He arrived at the Farmers' Club later than usual; do you remember what time he left here?'

'Same as always. You could set your clock by Billy; punctual to a fault, and expected everyone else to be.'

'So he left here when?'

'Ten to eight, same as always on club nights.'

Yet he had not reached the club till after nine. Allowing for twenty minutes' brisk walking, that still left fifty unaccounted for. Where had Billy Makepeace gone that evening, and had it any bearing on his death a few hours later?

According to Charlton, he had not been reported missing till the next day. Webb looked reflectively at the old woman's bent head. He said gently, 'You must have been worried when he didn't come home.'

'I didn't know till morning. I take sleeping pills, see; I'm always off by the time he gets back. But when I wakened he wasn't there. I called all over the house.' Her voice trembled, and with an effort she steadied it. 'I tried ringing the club but there was no reply, so I got on to the police.'

And an hour or so later, his body was found.

Webb got to his feet and replaced his chair against the wall. 'Thank you for seeing me, Mrs Makepeace. I hope it wasn't too painful for you. Sheila asked me to pass on her condolences. If there's anything she can do, just let her know.'

He nodded at Jackson and started towards the door, but the old woman's voice stopped him.

'David—Billy would have made it up long since, you know, if your dad had let him. He was right upset when John died. I mind him saying, "He shouldn't have gone without us shaking hands."'

Jackson tactfully went ahead into the hall. Webb said, 'So much bitterness, and I never even knew the cause of it.'

He waited hopefully, but the old woman's head had sunk on her chest and she'd retreated into a merciful doze. With a shrug Webb rejoined Jackson in the hall, and Jenny Hawthorn opened the front door for them.

'There's a farm manager, I believe,' Webb said. 'Where does he live?'

She nodded to the roof of the bungalow visible over the hedge. 'Over there. There might not be anyone home, though, at this time.'

'A Mr Croft and his wife?'

'That's right. They have three little girls.'

'We'll try our luck, while we're here. Thanks for your help, Mrs Hawthorn.'

She inclined her head and waited at the door until they turned out of the gateway on to the main road.

In fact, their luck held. As they walked up the drive next door, they could see Jerry Croft seated at a desk in one of the windows. He looked up at the sound of their footsteps, pushed back his chair and came to let them in. He was a tall, thin man in his late thirties, with black hair, small, alert brown eyes and red cheeks.

Webb identified himself and Croft led them inside to the room where they'd seen him working. It was furnished as an office, complete with closed-circuit television aligned on cowsheds and stables. Several businesslike filing cabinets stood against one wall, and there were open ledgers on the desk.

'How will this affect your job?' Webb asked, seating himself at the man's invitation.

A glance from the bright brown eyes showed Croft's awareness of the implications. 'I've not even thought about it, but provided Mrs Makepeace stays on, I imagine she'll still need me.'

'Did the old man take an active interest in the farm?'

'Very active. He was over first thing every morning, and often did the rounds with me. If it hadn't been for his heart, he'd never have given up the running of it.'

'You last saw him when?'

'Monday afternoon, from a distance. I was in the top field when he got back about five. I expected him to come up and join me but he didn't.'

'That was his usual practice?'

'Yes, he liked to have a rundown of the day's events, added to which there was a lamb we'd been concerned about. I was surprised he didn't come to check on it.'

The sound of a car turning into the drive made them glance out of the window. A white Peugeot drew to a halt outside and three small girls tumbled out of the rear doors clutching satchels and tennis racquets. The woman who'd been driving opened the boot and began to unload supermarket bags. She wore a neat white jacket and multicoloured skirt.

Webb resumed the interview. 'Were you aware of any ill-feeling towards Mr Makepeace?'

Croft shrugged. 'There are stories of a lifelong feud he'd waged with two local men, but I gather they're both dead now. When we first came we were told not to go to the Garden Centre, which is run by the daughter of one of them, nor the dairy owned by the other man's sons.' He gave a short laugh. 'In my opinion life's too short for nonsense of that kind, but he was the boss and I abided by the rules.'

'No more recent arguments or rows?'

'Not that I know of. He could be a cantankerous old devil, but basically he was a fair man, and people respected that. We'll all miss him.'

A few more routine questions followed, then the policemen took their leave.

'What we need to find out, Ken,' Webb said as they reached the gate, 'is when this absent-mindedness started —he seems to have been all right at lunch-time. Tell you what, you drive back and call on Jack Rogers—he's a timber merchant at the top of the High Street. Check that Makepeace actually did call, and what mood he was in. And if they remember seeing him at the library, all to the good. I'm going to walk back along the canal, tracing Billy's route. I want to refresh my memory of the surroundings and see if anything strikes me. I'll meet you at Silver Street in good time for the briefing.'

Jackson merely nodded. It seemed these solitary excursions of the Governor's were going to become a feature of this case. Resignedly he got into the car and started the engine.

Webb watched him drive away. Then he crossed the road to the dry scrubby grass and set off along the well-trodden footpath. On his left a hedge closed off the adjacent field, to his right poppies, daisies and dandelions speckled the coarse grass with colour. The path led up a slight rise and then dropped fairly steeply down to the water. As he followed it, the traffic on the road faded to a distant hum, like insects in the heavy air. Ahead, the canal lay waiting, serene and untroubled, its surface rippled only by the passage of a family of moorhens.

Webb drew a breath as past and present fused briefly in an uncomfortable time-warp. Then he stepped down on to the towpath and started walking back towards the town.

It was a different world down here, peaceful and unchanging. On the opposite bank a fisherman sat motionless, his line in the water, and memories stirred again. It was along this stretch that Webb had caught his first fish. He recalled bearing it triumphantly home; but when, as a surprise, his mother cooked it for him, he'd been unable to eat it. Staring at his plate, he could think only that the inert shape that lay there had that morning been full of life, swimming joyously in clear water. But for him, it would still have been, and to eat it would have choked him. He remembered his mother's bewilderment and his father's scorn.

Shaking himself free of the memory, Webb concentrated on the present, scanning the edges of the path for anything untoward. Everything looked so drowsy in the sunshine, so safe and timeless, that it was hard to remember a man had met his death here less than forty-eight hours ago.

He was approaching one of several bridges that gave access to farmland, and on impulse walked up its faded wooden planks and looked about him. A barge was rounding a bend some hundred yards ahead, and behind him the fisherman still sat unmoving. From this vantage-point he could see over the steep bank on the far side to stretching fields dotted with squat wooden pig-huts. Beyond, sheep moved ponderously, heads to the ground.

Eyes narrowed against the sun, Webb let his gaze move over the pastoral scene, and he felt the tightening in his chest before registering its cause. The old barn, where he and his friends had played as children, stood as it always had, its creosote faded, an odd plank missing, but for the most part unchanged, dark and brooding against the summer sky. There as small boys they had held gang meetings, picnicked on rainy days, hidden from authority. But though a refuge in early days, it became somewhere to avoid, a place of dread, of sinister secrets. He had not set foot in it for forty years, yet the sight of it still dried his mouth.

Aware that he was gripping the hand-rail, he forced himself to release it and, keeping his eyes on his immediate surroundings, returned to the towpath and continued his walk. And as he rounded the next bend the railway bridge came into sight, near which the body had been found.

Webb slowed his pace as he approached the scene of crime, aware of the painstaking searches which had taken place along this stretch. Though unlikely to find any fresh evidence, he was anxious none the less to form his own impressions. Firmly back in the present now, he moved from sunlight into the shadows of the bridge.

It was quite spacious under here, and the dark corners where the sun never reached smelled dank and cold. Plenty of room for an attacker to wait hidden in the darkness. Then what had happened? A quick shove from behind to knock the old man into the water, an uncompromising hand on the back of his head, holding him under?

Webb stood motionless for long moments, absorbing the feel of the place, imagining Makepeace, homeward bound and still preoccupied with whatever was troubling him, entering the deeper darkness and perhaps passing close by his killer. Did he see his face, and if so, would he have recognized it? More pertinently, did he, in those last agonized moments, know why he had to die?

Quite suddenly, Webb had had enough of his own company. He strode briskly out into the benison of the sunshine and within minutes reached the steps leading up to Bridge Street. The library clock was chiming four. An hour still to the briefing, but if he could track Jackson down, they could swap information over a cup of tea.

It was good to be back among the bustling life of the town, and now that he was on foot, Webb realized there had after all been changes. Basically, the old place had gone up-market. A rash of gift shops had sprung up, testifying to Broadshire's increasing share of the tourist trade, and on the corner where he'd bought his Saturday sweets The Body Shop now stood, its strange, exotic scents alien to his nostrils.

Little cobbled yards and alleys where, in his boyhood, tramps had scavenged among overflowing dustbins, were now freshly painted, and signposts invited passers-by to turn aside to visit tea-rooms, picture galleries or boutiques. No doubt about it, the place had been 'quaintified' but he supposed that, taken as a whole, it was an improvement.

There was also a proliferation of eating places, which would please Jackson. Tea-rooms, coffee shops, wine bars and carveries appeared on every side, and even the old-established hotels sprouted 'bistros' offering cheap and cheerful bar food.

And it was outside a café, wistfully regarding the cakes in the window, that he came across Jackson himself.

'I might have known!' he said, putting a hand on the sergeant's shoulder. 'Come on, we'll go in and sample the goods.'

CHAPTER 4

The journey back to Shillingham was effected in almost as deep a silence as the outward one had been, but at least Jackson now understood the Governor's reticence. Clearly, this case was likely to touch on his own past, and he couldn't be blamed for resenting it.

Webb himself, gazing out of the window, was brooding over the general outcome of the day. He now knew there had been two unusual occurrences on Billy Makepeace's last day of life: he had phoned Sheila and, though a stickler for punctuality, had arrived late at the Farmers' Club. Somehow, the explanation for both these facts must be ascertained.

In the meantime, Jackson's visits to both the timber merchant and the library had established that Makepeace had been his usual self, bargaining with Rogers over a needed length of fence, chatting to the librarian as she collected audio cassettes for his wife. And the times both had given, though approximate, tallied closely enough to assume that Makepeace had gone directly from one to the other.

Davis and Trent, detailed at the morning's briefing to visit the café, reported that as far as the waitress recalled, he'd arrived there shortly after four. Which meant, Webb reflected, gnawing on his lip, that he'd had little time for another call. So what had he seen or heard in that brief interval which had had an effect on him sufficiently profound to last throughout the evening and cause comment among his friends?

Webb sighed deeply and stirred, noting that they were approaching Shillingham. 'Drop me at home, Ken,' he remarked, 'I've had enough for today. You can take the car and collect me in the morning.'

'Right, Guv.'

It was six-thirty and the last of the rush-hour still clogged

Westgate. People queuing at the bus stop looked hot and tired; several men had removed their jackets, and a couple of children were crying. Ten to one, Webb reflected, the bus from the town centre would be full when it arrived. Poor sods.

Jackson turned into Fenton Street and came up Hillcrest from the lower end. As he drew up outside Beechcroft Mansions Hannah was approaching on foot from the other direction. Webb's spirits rose at the sight of her.

He got out of the car, aware of the shirt sticking to his back. 'Thanks, Ken. See you at eight-thirty.'

Jackson, hiding a smile, nodded and drove off, watching in the mirror as Miss James reached Webb and they turned together into the gateway. If the Governor believed their relationship was secret, far be it from him to disillusion him.

'You're late back,' Webb was remarking. 'I thought you teachers finished about three-thirty.'

'A common misapprehension,' she returned calmly. In pale lemon, she looked as cool and unruffled as she must have done first thing that morning. 'I presume you've spent the day in Erlesborough?'

'Correct.'

'Any joy?'

He grimaced. 'That's not a feeling I associate with Erlesborough. But as regards the investigation, no, it's far too early.'

'Did you have time to call on your sister?'

'Yes.' They had entered the hallway and were waiting for the lift.

Hannah said with a smile, 'As uncommunicative as ever!'

'No third degree, please, it's been the hell of a day. Look—' he reached a quick decision—'are you free this evening? Will you come out for a drink—or a meal, if you prefer?'

'A drink would be fine, David, but I've a couple of hours' work to do first. Could you call for me about eight-thirty?'

The lift stopped at her floor, she stepped out and Webb

continued to the one above, grateful that he wouldn't be faced with an evening's solitary introspection.

The Vernon brothers sat side by side on bar-stools in the Crown Hotel. Though they were not identical, there was a strong resemblance between them, accentuated by unconsciously shared mannerisms. In their late forties, both were of medium height with receding hairlines, but Tom was a stone heavier than his twin and Larry wore glasses.

'I hear Davy Webb's in charge of the case,' Tom said morosely. 'That's all we need.'

'No doubt he'll come nosing round the dairy,' Larry agreed.

'It's Ma I'm chiefly concerned about. If he starts questioning her, and he probably will, it'll start everything up again.'

'If you ask me, it's never far from her thoughts. I suspect some part of her's still waiting for Dad to come back.'

Tom swilled the beer in his glass. 'I'd give a lot to know what really happened. From what I remember, he seemed fond enough of us all. Why should he suddenly up and hop it?'

His brother shrugged. 'You know the facts as well as I do: business worries, Aunt Joan's illness and death. Stress *can* cause amnesia, and sometimes the memory never comes back. On the other hand, if he regained it later he might have decided he was better off where he was.'

Tom finished his drink and put the glass on the bar. 'Well, I must be getting along. Young Rich has a cricket match this evening and I promised to go and watch. See you.' He slid off the stool and made his way out of the bar. Larry sighed and ordered himself another pint. He'd a feeling the next few days were not going to be easy.

Jenny Hawthorn sat staring unseeingly at the television. Her eyes were smarting from a storm of weeping and her head ached. Across the hearth her mother dozed fitfully, still under the effect of the sedatives, and Jenny envied her her oblivion.

For the hundredth time her mind circled round the traumatic events of the last two days, returning again and again to a mental picture of herself and her father at La Brioche. Why hadn't she persisted in asking what was on his mind? And had whatever it was anything to do with his death? She'd never forgive herself if, by a little more questioning, she could have prevented it.

Painstakingly she went over their conversation once more, its banality endowed with significance as the last they had had together. But at the end of it, she admitted herself no wiser. He'd been so anxious to see her photos of his prize-winning ewe, that he'd asked her to slip out of the hotel to meet him. Yet when she produced them, he barely glanced at them.

But the point she kept coming back to, and which she had most difficulty in accepting, was that he had phoned Sheila Fairchild: Sheila, who, with the rest of her family, was enough of a pariah for her Garden Centre to be out of bounds to them. What could have caused such a total *volte-face*?

And from Sheila her thoughts went naturally to David, whose eyes, guarded, defensive, had been steadily on hers as he approached across the yard. Had he feared she'd refuse to see him?

Across the hearth the old woman stirred suddenly. 'Jenny?'

'I'm here, Mum.'

'Dad *did* make a phone call Monday evening—it's just come back to me. Two, in fact—the phone pinged a couple of times.'

Jenny shivered at this seeming confirmation of the impossible. 'Were they long calls?'

'No; I mind thinking both the folks he wanted must be out.' She paused, peering across at the indistinct shape of her daughter. 'You'd best let David Webb know.'

'Yes. Yes, I will.'

'Go on, then,' her mother urged, when she did not immediately move. 'It might be important.'

'I don't know where he is, Mum.'

'At the police station, where else?'

'All right, I'll try.'

She went out into the hall, flooded now with the last rays of the sun, and looked up the number in the directory. But when she got through, David had gone.

'Is it urgent?' a voice asked hopefully, when she identified herself.

'No, but it might be important. Could you ask him to contact me tomorrow?'

And as she went back to join her mother, she was aware of a small crumb of comfort in the desolation of her world. At least she'd have a chance to speak to David again.

There were Vernon's Dairies all over Broadshire, including at least two in Shillingham. Webb knew for a fact that Hannah shopped there for her special cheeses, but he had never himself been inside one. The idea that they were forbidden ground still lingered and the habit of avoiding them was ingrained in him. Today it was about to be broken.

The dairy's head office was in the building where the first shop had opened sixty years ago, in Erlesborough High Street, and it was there that Webb and Jackson went the next morning to interview the present directors. Webb was not looking forward to the meeting; the Makepeaces had been too distressed to show antagonism and he was, after all, trying to help them. With the Vernons, there would be nothing to breach the hostility of years.

The shop window, he noticed with grudging admiration, was set out like a museum showcase. Old-fashioned wooden implements flanked gleaming milk churns and cheese presses and there was an attractive display of terracotta butter moulds, while in pride of place stood a china model of a cow. Broadshire porcelain, by the look of it, and doubtless worth a bomb.

The interior, too, was impressive, more, thought Jackson, like a miniature food hall than somewhere one popped into for a pint of milk. There were glass counters holding every conceivable type of cheese, others with wide ranges of yogurts and cream desserts, and an American-style milk-bar along one wall. At the back of the shop stood a delicatessen counter and alongside it a cabinet labelled Home Made Dairy Ice-cream.

Obviously the worries which had beset poor Dick before his disappearance had been more than overcome and his sons ran a very thriving business.

'Can I help you, gentlemen?' The smart woman behind the cheese counter was smiling at them pleasantly.

'Is either of the Mr Vernons in?'

'I can check for you. Who shall I say?'

'Chief Inspector Webb, Shillingham CID.'

She showed no reaction, but two of the customers at the milk-bar turned and stared curiously. The assistant picked up a wall-phone and dialled a number. 'Chief Inspector Webb to see you, Mr Larry.'

Webb couldn't catch the reply, but the woman replaced the phone and opened a door behind her giving on to a flight of stairs. 'If you'd like to go up, sir.'

Grimly, with Jackson behind him, Webb complied. It was presumably Larry Vernon who awaited them at the top of the stairs, though Webb wouldn't have recognized him.

'You didn't waste much time,' he said by way of greeting, and before Webb could reply, turned on his heel and marched down the thickly carpeted corridor to a gleaming mahogany door which stood half-open. Without waiting for his visitors, he walked inside, crossed to an enormous desk and seated himself behind it. It was only as Webb followed him into the room that he saw the other brother by the window. United we stand, he thought ironically.

'You remember Tom, no doubt,' Larry said. 'Well, sit down and get it over. We're busy men.'

Jackson glanced at Webb, waiting for him to take control

of the interview. He'd been slow to do so, but then these two were, as far as the Governor was concerned, The Enemy, and the feeling was obviously mutual.

'I've one or two things to do myself,' Webb said acidly. 'I shan't keep you longer than necessary.' He looked at the two surly, middle-aged men, trying to see in them the small boys whose noses he had bloodied in the playground. And failed.

'We'll start with your addresses, if you'll give them to my sergeant here.' He waited while each man grudgingly complied. 'Now,' he continued, 'I'd like you to tell me, please, when you last saw Mr William Makepeace?' And as Tom made a movement, he added, 'Your brother first.'

Larry said impatiently, 'How do I know when I last saw him? It was always from a distance; as you know, we weren't on speaking terms.'

'Were you aware that he went to the Farmers' Club on Monday evenings?'

'No, I was not. I'd no idea what he did on Monday evenings, nor any other evening, for that matter. Furthermore, I didn't care.'

'Look, Mr Vernon, I appreciate this isn't easy for any of us, but your attitude's not helping.'

'I saw him,' Tom said unexpectedly. 'In the Crown, Sunday lunch-time. It's not his normal stamping ground, but he was with Gus Lang, the church organist.'

'Did he see you?'

'Yes. He turned his back, which saved my having to do so.'

Over Tom's shoulder, Webb could see the Crown Hotel immediately across the street. Presumably its clientele, along with the rest of Erlesborough, was aware of the long-standing feud.

'Apart from yourselves and my family, had anyone any ill-feeling towards him?'

'If so, they didn't discuss it with us,' Larry said drily.

'You haven't heard of any disagreements or resentments?'

'No.' Tom hesitated. 'To be fair, he was respected in the town. On the Bench, and all that. Even a churchwarden, for Pete's sake.'

'Where were you on Monday evening, Mr Vernon?'

Tom flushed darkly. 'Not lurking along the towpath, if that's what you're insinuating.'

'I'm not insinuating anything,' Webb said mildly.

'Then if you must know, I met some friends at the Crown.'

'Time?'

He shrugged. 'From eight till about eleven.'

Stapleton had not committed himself on the time of death, but it was likely to have been soon after Makepeace set off for home. Any time, in fact, between eleven and, say, eleven forty-five. Which did not clear Tom Vernon.

'And you, sir?' Webb turned to Larry.

'I was at the Cricket Club.'

'The whole evening?'

'Till about eleven. After the match we repaired to the bar.'

Some checking would be needed there, too.

Stung, perhaps, by Webb's impassivity, Larry burst out, 'Look, you surely don't think we'd anything to do with this? How would his death benefit us? We're not likely to be mentioned in his will!'

'It's purely routine at this stage, sir.' Webb paused, then asked casually, 'How's your mother keeping?'

'Extremely well, thank you, Chief Inspector,' said a crisp voice from behind him, and he turned quickly to see Mrs Vernon standing in the doorway. He rose to his feet as Tom said sharply,

'We asked you to stay in your room, Ma.'

'And I chose not to.' She looked Webb up and down. 'You've done well for yourself, David, no thanks to your father.' She walked into the room, and Webb awkwardly gestured towards the chair he'd vacated. She took it with a gracious nod. Apart from looking older, she was the same sharp-eyed woman he remembered. Adults didn't change, he reflected; it was the metamorphosis from childhood that was often unrecognizable.

'I'm still a director of the firm,' she told him. 'I come in at least twice a week to see how things are going. I was interested to see how you'd conduct this interview, and from what I overheard, you carried it off better than my sons did.'

'Really, Ma!' Larry shuffled papers irritably.

'And if you want to know where I was on Monday evening, I was at home, though I've no way of proving it. Nor am I going to say I regret Billy's death, because I don't.'

Webb smiled in spite of himself. 'That's refreshingly honest.'

'He was a stubborn, awkward old fool, with too high an opinion of himself. If Dick had been here, he'd have put an end to this farce years ago, but Billy and your father were too stiff-necked to budge.'

Webb, seizing the opening, said gently, 'You never heard from your husband, Mrs Vernon?'

He saw her quick tremor, instantly suppressed. 'No. Amnesia's often permanent, you know. I can only hope he's found happiness elsewhere.' She looked up, holding Webb's eyes with a steady gaze. 'He didn't leave me deliberately. I'm convinced of that.'

'I'm sure you're right, Mrs Vernon.'

She raised an eyebrow. 'Thank you. There were a number of sightings, mainly in the London area, but he'd always moved on by the time we got there.'

Webb would have liked to pursue the conversation. He'd his own reasons for hoping Dick was still alive, but it was not his disappearance they were investigating. Not, that is, unless he really had come back and topped his old rival which, after forty years, seemed unlikely.

'Well, I won't hold you up any longer. It might be necessary to see you again, but in the meantime, thank you for your time.' And, nodding to Jackson to follow him, he walked from the room, aware of three pairs of assessing eyes on his back.

Out on the pavement he turned to Jackson. 'I want a look at the café where the old man met his daughter. What was it called? Something fancy.'

Jackson consulted his notebook. 'La Bree-otch,' he said.

Webb snorted. 'In my day, we had Betty's Caff. Right, where is it, then?'

'Down near the Sandon Arms, Guv. I noticed it yesterday.'

That figured; Jenny had slipped out to meet her father. For a moment his mind lingered on her. He'd received her message on his arrival at Silver Street, and they'd arranged to meet in the Abbey Gardens at one. Slightly uneasily, he wondered what she wanted.

'And it's a good time for elevenses, and all,' Jackson was saying hopefully as they walked down the High Street.

'All right, we'll have a quick coffee when we've spoken to the waitress.'

La Brioche was a bit chi-chi for Webb's taste, and, he'd have thought, for Billy's. Jenny's choice, no doubt. There were check tablecloths in various colours, with matching crockery in each case. Their arrival had turned several heads—obviously they were not the usual type of customer —and a waitress approached to show them to a table. Webb produced his warrant card and asked his first question.

Her face sobered respectfully. 'Yes, sir. I remember the old gentleman.'

'Do you remember where he sat on Monday?'

'Yes, we've all been talking about it. It was that table down there, where the lady in the blue dress is.'

The table indicated was adjacent to those against the wall, with not much space between them.

'Who was at the nearest wall table?' Webb inquired.

'Three of my regular ladies, sir.'

'Do you know their names?'

'One's Mrs Fairchild, from the Garden Centre. I know, because I've seen her there.'

So Sheila was as close to Makepeace as that. 'I suppose you were pretty full?'

She looked surprised at his perception. 'Yes, we were. The gentleman asked if he could sit somewhere else, but there wasn't a space.'

'His daughter joined him later, I believe. Did anyone speak to him before she arrived?'

'Not that I saw, sir.'

'You didn't happen to hear what they were talking about? As you brought the tea, I mean,' he added hastily as she drew herself up.

'No, I didn't. I was too busy taking orders and serving to worry about that. We're short-staffed at holiday times and I was run off my feet.'

Not that she'd have admitted it if she had heard anything; they were within earshot of several tables and customers might get the wrong impression.

At what stage, Webb wondered, had Billy decided to phone Sheila? During tea, or afterwards? And, for God's sake, why?

Beside him, Jackson shifted from one foot to the other.

'Right,' Webb said to the girl, 'thanks for your help. While we're here, we'll have some coffee. And a couple of teacakes,' he added, as Jackson cleared his throat reprovingly.

'Certainly, sir. If you'd like to sit here?'

She showed them to a table near the empty fireplace, screened now by an arrangement of artificial flowers and feathers. Jackson, employing his powers of detection, asked tentatively, 'Would Mrs Fairchild be your sister, Guv?'

'She would indeed, Ken.'

'And the old man rang her later, though he'd never spoken to her?'

'That's right.'

'She didn't know why?'

'Couldn't imagine.'

'Might it have been because of something he heard her say?'

'Seeing how close the tables are, that possibility had occurred to me,' Webb said drily. 'When we've finished here, I'll give her a ring.'

Their coffee arrived, together with teacakes oozing butter, and, shelving their discussion, they settled down to enjoy them.

Webb phoned Sheila half an hour later, from Silver Street.

'I've just been to that Brioche place to see the lie of the land,' he told her. 'The tables are pretty close together, aren't they?'

'It's a popular place.'

'Who were you with on Monday?'

'Janet Conway and Angela Turner. I don't think you know them.'

'And old Makepeace was at the next table?'

'That's right.'

'Since he was alone at that point, he probably overheard your conversation.'

She was silent.

'So?' he prompted. 'What were you talking about?'

'All kinds of things,' she said evasively.

'Such as?' He was finding it hard to be patient with her. The fact that it was old Billy's death they were investigating was no excuse for her lack of cooperation.

She said unwillingly, 'Janet was telling us about a film she'd seen.'

His interest waned, but he asked perforce, 'What was it?'

'A ghost story of some kind. I don't remember the title. She said she'd been afraid to put the light out after seeing it.'

'What else did you talk about?'

'David, I can't remember!' she answered, with what seemed unnecessary vehemence. 'I really can't see the point of all this.'

He changed tack slightly. 'Well, did you notice if anyone approached old Makepeace, spoke to him?'

'No, I didn't.'

'How did he seem? Interested in what was going on, or deep in thought?'

'For heaven's sake! I didn't even know he was there till I looked up and saw him staring at me.'

'That's odd; I'd have expected him to pretend not to see you.'

Sheila said hurriedly, 'Look, I have to go—there's something on the stove.' And she put down the phone.

In her office off the kitchen, Sheila drew a deep breath. She knew she'd been unhelpful, knew David was annoyed with her. But she'd no intention of launching into that ghost business again. The dream had returned last night, and she'd woken this morning feeling like a wet rag. All she wanted was to consign it once and for all to oblivion. Anyway, she didn't for a moment believe Janet's contention that Mr Makepeace was interested in her story. Though, she remembered uncomfortably, he *had* phoned her that evening.

With an impatient shake of her head she returned to her lunch preparations.

'Not much help there,' Webb was reporting to Jackson. 'My sister and her friends were only discussing a film.'

'Perhaps the other ladies said something after she'd gone?'

'Then why didn't he phone them? They weren't involved in the feud.' Webb sat for a moment in silence, staring at the desk which had been assigned to him.

'All the same, Ken, it wouldn't do any harm to see them. Since they were still there when his daughter arrived, they might have overheard something. We'll get on to them after lunch. In the meantime, Mrs Hawthorn's asked to see me, so perhaps she'll tell me herself. I shouldn't be long, and while I'm tied up you can make yourself useful by doing a bit of alibi-checking at the Crown and the Cricket Club.'

CHAPTER 5

Emerging from Silver Street on to the High Street, Webb was directly opposite the archway leading to the Abbey Gardens. To his impatient amusement, his mouth was dry. It was, after all, nearly thirty years since he'd had a rendezvous with Jenny, and on the last occasion he'd been soundly beaten for it. It had proved to be the final straw, the deciding factor which crystallized his decision to leave home and join the police force. All in all, a meeting of some consequence.

Seeing a gap in the traffic, he crossed the road and made his way under the arch to the soothing greenery of the gardens. Immediately the noise and hassle fell away behind him and he felt himself relax. Lawns and flowerbeds stretched on all sides, and to his right lay the ruins of the Benedictine abbey which had once stood on the site.

He looked about him. On the seats, groups of girls sat eating their lunch and older women rested from their shopping. Several people, taking advantage of their lunch-hour to do some sunbathing, had spread themselves out on the grass. There was no sign of Jenny, and he was glad of the breathing space to marshal his thoughts.

Seeing her again yesterday had been oddly disturbing. She was, after all, his first love, Juliet to his Romeo, braving the wrath of their opposing families. And because they'd been forcibly separated, his feelings for her—and, who knew, perhaps hers for him—had not been allowed to wither naturally like most boy-and-girl affairs. She had remained his lost love, forbidden fruit, an object of unsatisfied desire.

Nor had she changed that much. In the edgy woman he had seen at Longacre, it was still possible to discern the young girl with her trusting eyes and sweet, oddly vulnerable, mouth.

He started to walk slowly down the path, aware of the various scents that reached him—nicotiana, pinks, mock orange. At the foot of the gardens the River Kittle wound its way under a small stone bridge, and some children were throwing bread to the ducks beneath.

He glanced at his watch, turned and started to walk back again, and it was then that he saw her hurrying through the archway, her dress a splash of vermilion as she came out of its shadows into full sunlight. He stopped, waiting for her to join him. She was wearing sunglasses, which afforded her a privacy he did not himself have.

'I'm sorry to have kept you,' she said breathlessly as she reached him. 'Someone phoned with a cancellation just as I was leaving.'

'No problem. Would you like to walk?'

'Yes, it might be—easier.'

He fell into step beside her, retracing the path he'd taken moments before. Around them, children played ball, dogs chased each other, old men dozed, but they walked in a silence of their own.

Breaking it, Webb said, 'You've something to tell me?'

'Yes. After you'd gone, Mother remembered that Dad did make two phone-calls on Monday.'

Webb glanced sideways at her. 'Two?'

She nodded. 'But both were brief, and she assumed he'd not got hold of whoever he wanted.'

'She doesn't know who he rang?'

'No, he used the upstairs phone. I don't suppose she was interested at the time; he made a lot of calls, what with church committees and his work on the Bench.'

'Assuming one was to Sheila, who was out, the other *could* have been successful, even if short. Confirming an appointment for that evening, say.'

'I suppose so,' she said doubtfully, 'but he was going to the club.'

'Yet he was late getting there, which was unusual. Since he left home at the normal time, he must have gone somewhere first.'

'I suppose so,' she said again.

'You've no idea where that could have been?'

'None at all.'

'It's important to find out, Jenny.'

'I realize that.'

They had reached a vacant seat, and by unspoken consent sat down. 'There's another thing I wanted to say,' she began diffidently.

'Yes?'

'You told Mother you didn't know the reason for all the trouble.'

'That's right.' His voice quickened. 'Do you?'

'Between Dad and the other two, yes, but that's only half of it. Dick and your father remained, if not friends, at least on speaking terms for a year or two after that.'

'There were two separate rifts? I didn't realize.'

'Well, as I say, I only know Dad's side of it. He told me years ago.'

There was a brief silence as Webb wondered whether, after all this time, he really wanted to hear it. Two, probably all three, of the men were dead. What did it matter now? But he heard himself say, 'What happened, then?'

She did not reply at once, and the air was filled with the sharp cries of a pair of ducks fighting over some bread. Webb watched them, the brilliant blues and greens of their plumage vivid in the sunlight. Then she said, 'When he was young, my father was an outstanding athlete. He specialized in sprinting and the long jump, and was chosen several times to represent England.'

Webb looked at her in surprise. 'I always remember him with a stick.'

'Yes.' She gave a deep sigh. 'As you know, the three of them were at school together, but although they were rivals, I gather there wasn't any real animosity. That started when they were twenty-one, and it was all so unnecessary, so *tragic!*' Her voice quivered.

Webb said nothing, waiting tensely at her side until she felt able to go on.

'They'd been to a party and they were very drunk. When it was time to go home, they all piled into a car—people thought nothing of it in those days. Of course, none of them was insured; Dick had borrowed his father's car without permission.

'Dad hadn't had as much as the others because he was in training and shouldn't have been drinking anyway. Well, there was a lot of fooling around, and he belatedly came to his senses and decided to get out and walk. But it was a two-door car and the others wouldn't let him out. They were in the front, laughing uproariously and fighting for the steering-wheel. The car suddenly started up and went careering off down the road.' She paused. 'You can guess what happened. They crashed sideways-on into a tree—it's a wonder they weren't all killed. The other two were hardly scratched, but Dad broke his leg in three places.' She paused, and added flatly, 'He'd just started training for the Olympics.

'Really, of course, they were all to blame, but Dad, beside himself at the collapse of his dreams, needed to lash out and the others were the obvious target. They were devastated at what had happened and tried several times to visit him, but he refused point-blank to see them. He was in hospital for months, and had to be represented when the court case came up. That was when it became very nasty, with accusations being hurled about and everyone blaming everyone else. But as far as Dad was concerned, the others had got off scot-free, while his entire life had been ruined.'

Webb was still watching the ducks. 'You're right, it is a tragic story; and it's being re-enacted, with slight variations, almost every day of the week.'

'He said he'd been ready to make it up years ago, but by then the other two were at daggers drawn and it was all too complicated.'

'How long ago did he tell you this?'

She said steadily, 'When you ran away from home.'

Webb digested that for a moment. 'Had he minded our seeing each other?'

She shook her head. 'I think he hoped it might bring him and John together.'

Webb said grimly, 'My father didn't see it that way. When he found out we'd been meeting, he took the strap to me.'

'Oh, David!' she said softly. 'I never knew. Was that why you left?'

'Partly; I went to Shillingham and found myself a job in a goods depot till I was old enough to join the police. I'd let Mother know where I was, so they could have come for me if they'd wanted. Obviously, they didn't. I never spoke to my father again.'

'That's—terrible.'

'Yes. I visited Mother several times when he wasn't there, but I was never very close to her, either. I didn't really get to know her till Father died and she went to live with Sheila and Colin.'

'He was a hard man, your father.'

He gave a harsh laugh. 'You don't have to tell me. Jenny, what did you do on Monday evening?'

The abrupt change of subject, from the past to the still more traumatic present, took her by surprise and she caught her breath.

'Monday? You mean when Dad—?'

'Yes. Where were you?'

'At home.' She added with a catch in her voice, 'I haven't got an alibi—I didn't realize I'd need one.'

'We have to check with everyone. Did you have any visitors or phone calls?'

'No. I came off duty at seven, went home, and spent the evening, like most others, entirely by myself. I knew nothing until Mum phoned the next morning to say Dad was missing.' She paused. 'But of course I can't prove it,' she added in a hard voice, and he realized the empathy between them had been wiped away. He regretted it, but it was outside his control.

He glanced at his watch. 'Well, I must be getting back to the station; my sergeant will be wondering where I am.

Thanks for meeting me, Jenny. It's good to see you again.'
And, leaving her still sitting there, he strode back up the
path towards the High Street.

After a late lunch, Webb and Jackson went to call on Janet
Conway, who, it turned out, lived in an attractive house
overlooking the golf course. Webb was pretty sure Sheila
wouldn't have mentioned their relationship, and had no
intention of revealing it himself. Her account should be
made to an investigating officer, not to the brother of a
friend.

She ushered them into a large, airy sitting-room with a
view of the fourth fairway, and produced afternoon tea in
china cups. While she bustled around, Webb took stock of
her, weighing her up as a potential witness. Small and
plump with fair, frizzy hair, she wore a pink blouse and a
linen skirt which strained slightly over her hips. In short,
she looked what she was, the contented wife of a successful
businessman.

Having seen to the needs of her guests, she settled herself
in an armchair and looked across at him, meeting his gaze.
It did not appear to disconcert her.

'Now, Chief Inspector,' she said, 'how can I help you?'

'As you'll have gathered, Mrs Conway, we're investigating the death of Mr William Makepeace. How did you hear
of it, by the way?' It was she, he remembered, who had
told Sheila.

'From Vera Adams, the doctor's wife. She'd left a scarf
in my car when I ran her home from WI, and I dropped it
in on my way to the shops.'

He nodded. 'I believe you saw Mr Makepeace the day
he died?'

'My goodness, that does sound sinister! I suppose you
mean in the café? Yes, he came in while we were there.'

'Did you notice anything unusual about him? Was he
distracted or upset in any way?'

She smiled. 'All I noticed, Chief Inspector, was that he

was most intrigued by our conversation. His eyes were positively on stalks!'

Webb kept his voice casual. 'And what were you talking about?'

'Ghosts, actually. I'd been to the cinema the previous evening and seen a pretty hair-raising film, and I was telling my friends about it. Angela—Mrs Turner, that is—pooh-poohed the whole thing, and said it was stupid to be frightened by a ghost story when such things didn't exist. And then my other friend, Mrs Fairchild, said that they *did* exist, and what was more she'd seen one!'

There was total silence. Then, 'Mrs Fairchild said she'd seen a ghost?'

'That's right. She told us the whole story—and I don't wonder the old man was riveted, I was on the edge of my seat myself. You see, Sheila's the most down-to-earth person imaginable—it was so unexpected.' She gave a little laugh. 'I should have known better; the next day she confessed it had been a joke, to take Angela down a peg.'

'But you believed her at the time?'

'Totally. She was so convincing.'

'And you think Mr Makepeace did too?'

'I'm sure of it. But—well, you wouldn't know, but there's been bad feeling for years between Mrs Fairchild's family and the Makepeaces, and as soon as she saw him staring at her, she picked up her handbag and left. She hadn't even finished her tea.'

'When was she supposed to have seen this ghost?'

'Oh, years ago, when she was little. It gave her nightmares for years, she said. But I suppose that was also part of the leg-pull.'

Nightmares. He'd forgotten all about them, but now the memory flooded back of those years when Sheila's bad dreams had disrupted the whole family; when, overnight it seemed, she had changed from a carefree little girl into a timid, clinging child afraid to leave her mother's side. At the time, it was suggested that—

Webb's thoughts skidded to a startled halt. Mrs Conway

was staring at him and he hastily collected himself. She said with a half-laugh, 'For a moment there, Chief Inspector, you looked as if you'd seen a ghost yourself!'

He forced a smile. 'And Mrs—Turner, was it? How did she react to the story?'

'She says she knew Sheila was stringing us along, but I don't believe her.'

Webb tried to anchor his spinning thoughts. 'Did Mr Makepeace repeat it to his daughter?'

'I don't think so. She seemed to do all the talking, he just sat there.'

'So what *was* the story?'

'It sounds too silly for words now. Something about a figure rising out of a grave. I should have realized it was a hoax.'

Time enough to analyse that later. 'Did anyone else speak to Mr Makepeace while he was in the café, either before or after his daughter joined him?'

She shook her head positively. 'No, I was facing the door and saw him arrive. He didn't want to take that table—I suppose because it was so close to Sheila—but there was nowhere else.'

So as far as could be deduced, Makepeace had arrived in good spirits direct from the library, listened to Sheila's ghost story, and become so preoccupied that he'd shown no interest in Jenny's photographs which were the reason for their meeting. On the face of it, it didn't make sense. And yet . . .

Sitting there in that pleasant room, a cup of tea in his hand, Webb admitted to himself that for the first time in his life he was involved in a case he did not want to solve. He finished his tea and put the cup down. 'Thank you very much, Mrs Conway, you've been most helpful.'

'Have I?' She sounded surprised, as well she might, and once in the car, Jackson echoed her doubt.

'That sounded like a lot of baloney to me,' he remarked. 'You don't really think the old boy was interested in a ghost story, do you, Guv?'

'The point is, Ken, that whether she thought she saw a ghost or not, my sister certainly suffered from nightmares.'

'Well, most kids do,' Jackson said reasonably.

'Occasionally, I dare say, but these changed her whole character. They started when she was five, and she was still having the odd one in her teens. The house was in a continual uproar, with her screaming and crying.'

'When you asked her what they'd been talking about,' Jackson said diffidently, 'did she mention saying she'd seen a ghost?'

'No, she did not.'

The tone of Webb's voice intimated it would be unwise to pursue the subject, but after a moment he added, 'I'll have to look into it, obviously, if only for elimination purposes.' He reached for the phone and dialled The Old Farmhouse. It was his brother-in-law who answered.

'Sorry, David, Sheila's not here; she's gone over to Heatherton for some supplies. Is it urgent?'

'I would like to see her, to clear up a few points.'

'She won't be back till about six. Why not join us for supper? Stay the night, if you like.'

'No, really, I don't want to put you to any trouble.'

'No trouble at all. It would give us the chance for a good chat, and you could relax instead of having to dash back to Shillingham.'

'Shouldn't you check with Sheila first?' Though she'd already issued a general invitation.

'Nonsense!' said Sheila's husband roundly. 'There's plenty of food, and as you know, the guest-room's always ready. I can provide a razor and pyjamas, so all you have to do is buy a toothbrush! Come whenever you like; we usually eat at seven.'

'Right, Colin, thanks. I'll see you then.'

'So where now, Guv?' Jackson asked, as Webb slid the phone back under the dashboard. 'Do you want to check with that other woman, Mrs Turner?'

'Not for the moment, we'll wait and see what my sister has to say. In the meantime, we'll look in at Silver Street and see if the action teams have come up with anything. We've an hour in hand before the briefing, so we can make use of it by getting our notes up to date.'

At the Garden Centre, Colin Fairchild went back to setting out furniture in the show conservatory. It was shaded from the sun by one of the buildings and the sliding door was wide open, but the atmosphere inside was stifling.

As he moved the chintz-covered chairs about and arranged glossy magazines on a table, his thoughts were still on his brother-in-law. They'd known each other since primary school, but lost touch when he himself became a weekly boarder at Greystones instead of going to Shillingham Grammar like the rest of them.

A nice enough chap, David, but hard to get to know, which was probably due to his background. Both he and Sheila had suffered lasting damage from the disaster that was their parents' marriage. Colin was well aware that the reason his wife drove herself so hard was that she was determined to be as unlike her mother as possible. She had decided at an early age that her own marriage would be quite different—equal strengths, shared decisions and responsibilities. He worried that she did so much—working alongside himself and Stephen at the Centre, running the house, baking bread and cakes for sale in the coffee shop and cooking the lunches which were served there at weekends. But it was useless to suggest she slowed down.

In addition, she dealt with the purchase and sales ledgers, made up the wage packets and carried out a number of local deliveries. And away from the Centre, he'd lost count of the number of committees she was on. Such ferocious efficiency did not make her easy to live with, and he often wondered how long it would take her to prove herself. It was indeed a heavy burden her parents had unwittingly laid on her.

Colin paused to survey the layout, but his thoughts were on the old couple, on John, stern and unbending, given to explosions of unreasonable anger, and Lilian, weak,

subservient, permanently discontented. It would be hard
to have found a couple less suited to have children. John,
while idolizing his little daughter, had been unfairly hard
on his son, and Lilian too dispirited to show much interest
in either of them. And as if that wasn't bad enough, there'd
been that ridiculous feud.

Which brought him back to Makepeace's death. He
straightened, wiping the back of his hand across his forehead. It was an unpleasant business, and during the course
of it a good many stones were likely to be turned over,
revealing facts which would better have remained hidden.
For the first time, he wondered uneasily just how good a
policeman David was.

'Dad—' Stephen put his head through the open doorway. 'Some people are interested in the round summer-
house. Could you come?'

'Be right with you.' And, locking the conservatory behind
him, he also turned the key on the disquieting possibilities
which had presented themselves. Time enough to worry
about those if they materialized.

Sally Croft stood in her kitchen, trying to analyse her feelings. They were more complex than she could have wished,
since she was happiest when everything, including emotions, could be neatly labelled and filed.

Mr Makepeace's death had been a shock, naturally, but
her reactions even to that were ambivalent. Her immediate
thought, somewhat to her shame, had been how it would
affect them. Suppose the old girl sold up and moved in with
her daughter? A new owner might not require a manager,
even one as conscientious and hard-working as Jerry.
Which would mean having to move, the very last thing she
wanted to contemplate.

In the two years they'd lived at Longacre, Sally had made
a very pleasant little niche for herself, not least in her job
at St Gay's. Being in the same building as the children
was convenient, as was the fact that her holidays coincided
exactly with theirs. What was more, all three were making

good progress, and Ruth would be starting at Shillingham Grammar in September. If they had to move now, there was no saying where Jerry'd find another job. It might not even be in Broadshire, and there'd be all the upheaval of finding new schools and trying to get a place for herself.

As to the old man himself, she'd hardly known him. She had, however, resented on Jerry's behalf the continual overseeing of everything he did. The point, surely, of employing a manager, was to take the burden off oneself. But old man Makepeace had been unable to let go the reins, and was forever following Jerry round, looking over his shoulder and even, on occasion, countermanding his orders to the men.

Then there was the business of the loan. Sally had been strongly against Jerry's asking for it, but since the bank wouldn't help them, there'd been no alternative. Even with her salary, there was no way they could afford to keep Jerry's mother in the only nursing home to have room for her. But the repayment, together with interest—for Makepeace had been a shrewd businessman—was a constant millstone which, though she hated herself for it, she resented.

Suppose his widow was advised by her solicitor to call in the loan? Though she would certainly not be short of money, he might feel she could get a better return elsewhere. Or—another possibility and maybe a more likely one—perhaps the old lady wouldn't long survive her husband. And if that were the case, there was no saying how Mrs Hawthorn would feel about the loan. In fact, Sally thought, there was no knowing how Mrs Hawthorn felt about anything.

'Is tea ready, Mummy?' Rebecca was swinging on the door handle, watching her curiously. Sally became aware that the basket of groceries was still on the table and she hadn't even started to unpack it. Consciously she unclenched her hands and smiled at her daughter.

'It won't be long, darling. You can lay the table for me.'

It wasn't until she had served the children and was preparing supper for Jerry and herself that another thought struck Sally. Perhaps the fact about their employer's death that should cause her most concern was that it had not been a natural one. Someone, somewhere, had wanted Mr Makepeace out of the way.

CHAPTER 6

It was half past six when Jackson dropped Webb off at The Old Farmhouse, with instructions to collect him first thing in the morning. The dog Jason came bounding up to meet him, his tail waving.

'Hello, old boy.' Webb stooped briefly to pat him, and when he straightened, saw Sheila in the open doorway. 'I hope this is all right,' he said awkwardly. 'Colin insisted it would be.'

'You've an open invitation—I told you. Supper won't be long, but if you'd like a wash first, go straight up. Your room's ready for you.'

'Thanks.'

'And if the cat's on the bed, throw him off,' she called after him as he started up the stairs.

He pushed open the door of the room that was allotted to him each Christmas, noting that the cat was indeed curled up on the bed, but feeling its right to be there was greater than his. It was a room he'd occupied only in winter, and he was surprised at the change the season made. Now, filled with sunlight, the sprigged curtains looked fresh and summery and the window was open to a garden bright with flowers.

Webb had always suspected that the Christmas invitations were issued more out of duty than over-riding affection. When he first left home and joined the police, he'd made a point of volunteering for Christmas duty as an excuse for not going home. Then came the eleven years of his marriage, during which he hardly saw his family. The present arrangement had begun four years ago when, after his father's death, his mother moved to The Old Farmhouse, and it had evolved into a tradition neither he nor Sheila knew how to break. Perhaps, basically, they didn't want to. Now, he found himself hoping that his questioning on the ghost story would not cause any new ripples between them. The trouble with this case, Webb told himself, not for the first time, was that it evoked altogether too much soul-searching.

Resolutely pushing it aside, he had a quick wash at the basin, noting the fresh smell as he buried his face in the towel. Country air, he thought appreciatively; very different from the odourless, laundry-washed towels at home. Colin had been as good as his word; an electric razor stood on the shelf above the basin, and a quick look under the pillow revealed a pair of neatly folded pyjamas. He took out his new toothbrush, cleaned his teeth vigorously, and went downstairs to join his family.

Of them all, he felt most comfortable with his nephew. The boy was pleasant, uncomplicated and friendly, and more than once it had crossed his mind that it would be good to have a son like Stephen. Not that it was any use going down that track.

With Sheila, perhaps unfairly, he felt he was walking on eggshells, and Colin had always been at one remove. He remembered the defensive scoffing of himself and his pals when they learned that instead of accompanying them to grammar school, the solicitor's son would be going to the rarified environs of Greystones College. Later, it was said openly that Sheila Webb had done well for herself in catching him, even though by that time, strongly against his father's wishes, Colin had dropped out of university to open the Garden Centre.

As for Lyn, Webb freely confessed he didn't know how to treat young girls. Those he came regularly into contact with were of the criminal sorority, up for shoplifting or worse, their language, to his private distaste, as colourful as that of the lads. Girls like his niece were an unknown quantity, and to his annoyance he felt embarrassed in her presence.

She was draped in an armchair now, a textbook open on her knee but her eyes on the television set. She looked up as Webb walked hesitantly into the room. 'Hi,' she said.

'Hello.' As he stood awkwardly, Stephen came in behind him, and he felt the boy's hand on his shoulder.

'Hello, Uncle! Good to see you—Christmas is early this year!'

Webb turned with a smile. 'Good to see you, too, Stephen. How are things?'

'OK. Busy as usual. Are you having any luck on the Makepeace case?'

Typical Stephen, no dissembling.

'It's early days yet,' he said evasively, and his eyes returned to Lyn. 'I believe you took his call on Monday?'

'That's right.'

'Could you tell me exactly what he said?'

'Just, "Is that Mrs Fairchild?" I said no, and who was speaking, and when he gave his name I nearly flipped. I told him Mum was out and could I take a message, but he said it didn't matter and put down the phone.'

Which was just as Sheila had reported it. Damn; he'd hoped for an extra something which could have been significant.

Supper was eaten round the dining table, though Webb suspected that without his presence it might have been partaken of in the kitchen. It seemed to have been tacitly agreed that any questioning should wait till after the meal, and he was happy that this should be so. If her son and daughter were present, Sheila might have even more reservations about retelling her story.

The evening had clouded over, and grey clouds were banking in the sky. Perhaps there'd be a break in the weather. 'If only it'd rain,' Colin said, 'it would save us setting up the hoses. It's the devil of a job, I can tell you, seeing everything has enough water.'

Webb thought fleetingly of Mrs Taverner in the garden at

Beechcroft. Doubtless she would also welcome a downpour.

The meal ended and both young people excused themselves, Lyn to go and study in her room, Stephen, with an anxious eye on the weather, to play tennis.

'You men go through while I tidy away,' Sheila said briskly. 'I'll bring the coffee in a few minutes.'

Obediently they walked through to the sitting-room, dim in the darkening evening. Again, the room had a different persona from the one Webb was used to, when a Christmas tree stood in the corner and logs blazed in the grate. Now, vases of flowers were dotted about and the chairs and sofa were grouped to face the windows.

As they seated themselves, Colin said abruptly, 'It can't be easy for you, this case.'

'Like probing a sore tooth,' Webb admitted.

Colin hesitated, then asked with studied casualness, 'Have you seen the Vernons yet?'

Webb's quickened interest was not apparent in his voice. 'Yes, I called at the dairy. Their mother was there too.'

'Could they possibly have a hand in this?'

'Colin, at this stage anyone could.'

'I've been racking my brains, but I honestly can't think of anyone who'd gain from old Billy's death. Nor can I imagine he was a threat to anybody.'

'Obviously someone didn't agree with you.'

'It wasn't just a random mugging?' Colin asked almost hopefully.

'No, nothing was taken.'

Stephen's footsteps came running down the stairs. ''Bye!' he called. 'I should be back about ten.' The front door slammed behind him, followed a moment later by the sound of a motorbike starting up.

'Sheila hates it when he's out on that thing,' Colin said.

Webb wished his sister would appear. Conversation was becoming increasingly stilted, both men tacitly acknowledging they were marking time before the point of Webb's visit was revealed.

She came at last, bearing a tray of coffee cups which she

set down on the low table in front of them. Beyond the window, the sky had darkened still further over the canal and there was a dull yellow heaviness in the air.

Sheila poured the coffee, handed round the cups, and settled back in her chair, tucking her feet beneath her. 'Well, David, I gather you've some more questions for me?'

'Yes.' He took a sip of coffee. 'I went to see Mrs Conway this afternoon.'

She tensed. 'Why on earth?'

'Everything in a murder case has to be checked and double-checked. I wanted her impression of how Billy had seemed in the café.'

'And you discovered,' Sheila said in a low voice, 'that the film wasn't the only thing we talked about.'

Colin frowned. 'What do you mean?'

Webb kept his eyes on his sister. 'So I'd like the full story this time, please.'

'I suppose I've no choice.' Her voice was bitter. 'Not that I can see it has the faintest relevance to the case.'

'Makepeace overheard you and later, breaking the habit of a lifetime, he tried to phone you. Doesn't that strike you as relevant?'

'*What* did Makepeace overhear, for God's sake?' Colin interrupted. 'Will someone tell me what this is about?'

'Sheila and her friends were discussing ghosts.'

'*Ghosts?*' Colin gave a disbelieving laugh.

'And Sheila said she'd seen one.'

Colin stared at his wife in amazement. 'Is this true?'

'That I said so, or that I saw one? Look, all right—' as both her husband and brother moved protestingly—'I knew this'd come up. But it's a long story.'

'We've got all night,' Webb said.

A sudden spatter of rain rattled against the windows, and large drops began to darken the stone patio.

'It's to do with your nightmares, isn't it?' he prompted.

Colin looked blankly from one to the other, but they ignored him.

'Yes.' Sheila finished the coffee in her cup and refilled all

three, to the men's impatience. Then she settled back again.
'It started on my fifth birthday. We'd had a picnic tea in
Piper's Wood, and at bedtime I realized I'd left my teddy-
bear behind. I never went to bed without it and was all set
to go back for it, but they wouldn't let me. I pleaded and
cried, but to no avail.'

She looked at Webb with a half-smile. 'You didn't help
—you said it would be eaten by foxes. I yelled even louder,
but was told I'd have to wait till morning, and that was
that. I cried myself to sleep, but later, when it was dark,
something woke me. I got out of bed and saw a light under
your door.'

She looked at Webb, who was sitting rigidly staring at
her, his coffee forgotten. Of course—it tied in.

'So, since I was awake, I decided to go and rescue my
bear. The darkness outside didn't bother me. I *was* a bit
chary of the bogeyman, which Mum was always saying
would get me if I was naughty, but he came in the pleasantly frightening category of witches and dragons, one step
from reality. So—' she drew a deep breath—'I pulled a
jumper and trews over my pyjamas and crept downstairs
with my shoes in my hand. We never used the front door,
if you remember.' Oh, he remembered. 'The key'd been
lost years ago and it was kept permanently bolted. Still, I
managed to open it without any difficulty.'

A low rumble of thunder broke suddenly, making all
three jump. 'Sound effects!' Sheila said. 'Well, no one was
about. There was a full moon and it was fairly bright. I
crossed Lower Road and walked the short distance to
Chapel Lane. As you know, Piper's Wood is about half a
mile down it, on the right. And on the left is the cemetery.'
She shuddered suddenly, slopping the coffee in the saucer,
and, leaning forward, put it on the table.

'It's no use saying I imagined this,' she said jerkily. 'How
could I? I'd never heard of ghosts, and I didn't know what
a cemetery was. But as I walked along, intent on reaching
the wood, something the other side of the hedge caught my
attention. There were odd gaps between the branches and

I stopped and peered through. And—and that was when I saw it—a figure rising up out of a grave.'

'Oh, Sheila, come on!' Colin protested.

'I swear it!' Her hand clenched on the arm of her chair. 'It was so close—just the other side of the hedge. I was convinced it was the bogeyman, after me because I'd disobeyed Mum. I rushed home, bolted the door again—as though that would keep him out!—and fled back to bed.'

'And the next morning,' Webb said, remembering with painful clarity, 'you hid under the bedclothes and screamed when Mother tried to drag you out. That was always reckoned to be the start of your nightmares.'

'It was, only that first time it was real. For years I believed it was the bogeyman I'd seen, and that since I'd escaped he'd still be looking for me. And night after night I dreamt he caught me.'

'You never told me about these dreams,' Colin accused her.

She barely heard him, still caught up in her memories. 'I suppose I was twelve or thirteen when it struck me that what I'd seen must have been a ghost. Not that it was any comfort. I tried to tell Mum at that point, but she wouldn't listen. She said it was wicked to tell lies and God would punish me.' She laughed tremulously. 'God instead of the bogeyman; out of the frying-pan—'

Webb leaned forward. 'Sheila, you say this figure was just the other side of the hedge. You must have had a pretty good view of it.'

She shuddered.

'Well?' he prompted. 'What did it look like?'

'You honestly expect me to know? Like—like the bogeyman, for God's sake!'

'Please, Sheila, this could be vital. Try to see the figure again now, through adult eyes. Can you describe it?'

She concentrated for a moment, and he could see she was trembling. His bossy, efficient sister was still not free from childhood terrors, and the realization softened his feelings for her.

'Well?'

She drew a breath. 'All I can say is, it was—black.'

'You said there was a moon.' As he, too, remembered.

'Then it must have been behind him.'

'You couldn't distinguish any features?'

'David, I didn't try! I fled.'

He sat back, resigned that he wouldn't get any more out of her.

She said suddenly, 'You were out that night, weren't you? It would have been you coming upstairs that woke me. Where'd you been?'

It was pointless to deny it. 'To the old barn.'

'Whatever for?'

'To spy on Beth Jones and Trevor Pitt, who did their courting there. Harry Davis had dared me. But they didn't come and I fell asleep and didn't wake up till it was dark.'

Almost true, as far as it went. Fortunately it satisfied Sheila, and she accepted his explanation with a smile.

Colin, breaking into the exclusiveness of their shared memory, said forcefully, 'I'm damned if I see what this has to do with Billy Makepeace.'

Webb turned to him. 'I've a feeling his death is only one of our problems. We also need to know what happened to Dick Vernon forty years ago.'

Sheila frowned. 'Mr Vernon? But—'

'You do realize, don't you, when it was that he disappeared?'

She stared at him. Then she said, just above a whisper, 'On my fifth birthday.'

Webb turned to Colin. 'Overnight, as you'll have gathered, she turned from a happy, fearless child to a bundle of nerves, crying and screaming at the slightest thing. It was put down to insecurity—fear that her own father might go away too.'

Sheila said, 'And this week the dreams have come back. I suppose it was going through it all in the café.'

'That's why you went downstairs that night?' Colin asked her. 'Why ever didn't you tell me?'

'I didn't want to talk about it, or even tell David, unless I had to. I just wanted to forget it as soon as possible.'

Webb said, 'When you told the story in the café, did you put any date on it?'

'I just said forty-odd years ago.'

'But even if Makepeace did overhear it,' Colin said, 'why on earth should he want to speak to you?'

Before his wife could reply, Webb broke in. 'Do you remember which grave it was?'

'For pity's sake!' Colin exploded. 'Surely *you* don't believe in ghosts?'

'I believe Sheila saw something, and I intend to find out what—or who. What do you think, Sheila? Could you pick it out?'

The room lit suddenly in a weird glow of lightning, plunging back to gloom as thunder crashed directly overhead. Stephen wouldn't be getting much tennis this evening.

Sheila considered his question. 'I don't know. Possibly, since it was near the hedge.'

'I'd like you to try, first thing in the morning.'

'What is it, David? You've an idea, haven't you?'

'I'll tell you tomorrow, provided I'm right. And if I am, I don't think the dream will worry you any more. Though my troubles will be just beginning.'

By mutual consent, the subject wasn't discussed any further. They sat in silence for a while, watching the rain sheet down on to the parched earth and flinching at the occasional clap of thunder. Then Colin switched on the television, and it was relief to sit back and let something else fill their minds.

Webb was not sorry when it was bedtime, but he didn't sleep well. Sheila's story and its possible significance circled continuously in his head, together with his own experiences on that night, which, for forty years, he had striven to suppress.

He shouldn't have taken this case: he should have insisted to the Chief Super that he was too personally involved. But how could he have known it would blow up in his face like this?

After tossing and turning for several hours he was uncomfortably hot, and got up to go and sit by the window. The summer night was already lightening and the sky fading to duck-egg blue, calm and new-washed from the storm. Already birds were stirring in the trees by the canal. He sat and watched them for some time, soothed by the unchanging cycle of day following night. Then, having no dressing-gown, he began to feel chilly and returned to bed, where he fell at last into a deep sleep, from which Sheila woke him with a cup of tea at seven-thirty.

He looked up at her blearily. 'No dreams, I trust?'

'No sleep!' she replied. 'Well, not strictly true. I did doze a bit.'

'I was much the same. I didn't drop off till around dawn.'

'You still want me to go to the cemetery with you?'

'Yes indeed. My sergeant will be collecting me at eight forty-five. We can go straight down, if that's convenient?'

'It isn't very, but I suppose police business has to come first. Friday's my baking day: a dozen cottage loaves, a dozen wholemeal, four dozen scones and six jam sponges.'

He stared at her, aghast. '*Every* Friday?'

'Every Friday—most are regular orders. Actually I've done the first batch, but there's also the weekend lunches to prepare, roughly three dozen a day. I only do those in the summer.'

'And I thought I worked hard! We won't keep you long, I promise.'

'You really think it's significant, what I saw all those years ago?'

'I think it might well be.'

She held his gaze for a moment, then nodded and turned to leave the room. 'Breakfast in half an hour?'

'Fine. Thanks.'

He showered, shaved with the borrowed razor, and felt marginally more human. There was a long day ahead of him, and he wondered uneasily what he would have discovered by the end of it.

Jackson, arriving at the time stipulated, was surprised to
see a woman coming through the gate with the Governor.
Webb introduced them briefly. 'I want you to drive us to
the cemetery, Ken. We can get to it along Bridge Street—
I'll direct you.'

The Governor got into the back of the car with his sister.
In the rear-view mirror both of them looked serious, and
Jackson forbore from any questions as he turned the car
and headed back towards town. The drive took them past
the Farmers' Club and over the canal bridge where Makepeace had descended to the towpath on his last night of life.
At the T-junction they turned left into Lower Road, and,
after a few hundred yards, right into Chapel Lane. The
cemetery bordered the road to the left.

'Want me to drive in, Guv?'

'No, just park here. There's no need for you to get out,
Ken; we'll be driving my sister back in a few minutes.'

Sheila was already on the pavement, looking over the
hedge at the depressing expanse of gravestones. As David
joined her, she said, 'I've been here several times over the
years; it's hard to remember how it was that night.'

'Close your eyes and try to think back.' He waited, giving
her a few minutes. Then, 'How far had you come when you
heard the noise?'

She opened her eyes and looked to left and right, shrugging helplessly. 'I really can't be sure. It's all so different.'
She waved a hand, embracing hundreds of graves to the
right. 'For instance, all this was grass.'

'Good, you've started to remember. Now, which grave
did the figure emerge from? It was in this row alongside the
hedge, wasn't it?'

She turned again, looking back to the top of the lane to
estimate the distance from the corner. Then she took a few
tentative steps, first one way and then the other, checking
the gravestones as she did so. Webb watched her in silence,

aware of Jackson's curiosity as he witnessed the performance from the car.

Eventually Sheila stopped and turned to face him. 'I must have been about here,' she said. 'Within a few feet either way.'

'Good. We'll go in and see whose are the nearest graves. Then we can check with the burial register which were new that day.'

'You think it was a new grave?'

'It would have to be a pretty strong ghost if it wasn't,' Webb said with grim humour.

They went through the cemetery gates and turned to walk along the bottom row of graves. After a moment Webb said, 'This is just about the place. So who have we got here?' He read the headstone. 'In memory of Harold Fuller who died March 30th 1951 aged 79 years. Right year, anyway. We'll memorize the next half-dozen, then check the burial dates.'

Together they moved slowly along, noting the names on the next few graves. Mason, Davis, Jones, Wainwright—

Webb halted so suddenly that Sheila bumped into him. 'Look at this,' he said grimly. 'Joan Wainwright, dearly loved wife of Samuel—'

He turned to look into Sheila's wide eyes. 'You remember who she was?'

'Of course. Dick Vernon's twin sister.'

'Whose death was supposed to have caused his amnesia. Come on, let's look in the register.'

He took her arm and walked her quickly back to the main path which led up the centre of the cemetery. The whole area was beautifully kept; the tombstones were clean and white, nearly every one decorated with flowers, and the newly mown grass glinted with the previous night's rain. A peaceful resting-place, he thought—at least, it should have been.

Over to their left a man was tending one of the graves and they walked across to join him. Webb produced his warrant card and the man straightened.

'Yes, sir. What can I do for you?'

'I presume you keep a burial register here?'

'That's right, in the chapel up top.'

'How far back do your records go?'

'Well, now, let's see.' The man scratched his head. 'I reckon the earliest we have here is for 1920. Before that, you'd need to go to the county archives.'

'That's well within our limit. We'd like to know the burial dates for some of the graves along the hedge down there.'

'Right, sir, if you'll come with me we'll have a look-see.' Wiping his hands down his trousers, he set off with them towards the small building at the top of the site. It was, Webb thought, an insignificant little chapel to have lent its name to the lane. But he remembered hearing that, years ago, the inhabitants of some cottages further along had objected to living in Cemetery Lane and the name had been changed.

Small, dusty and seldom used, the chapel housed a lawn-mower, and a hoe was propped against one wall. The man went ahead of them to the tiny vestry leading off it, where he produced his books of records.

'Down by the hedge, you said.' He glanced up at the framed plan of the cemetery which hung on the wall. 'Left or right of the gate?'

'Left.'

'That'll be Section B. What name was it, sir?'

Webb looked at Sheila. 'Mrs Joan Wainwright. You might try 24th May 1951.'

The caretaker selected the appropriate book and turned over pages filled with copperplate handwriting. 'Here we are, sir. Almost spot-on.'

Webb and Sheila bent quickly forward. There was only one entry for that week. It read: '*Joan Elizabeth Wainwright of Lansdown Road, Erlesborough. Aged 38. Section B, grave space 323. Interr. Wed. May 23rd 1951 at 3.30p.m. Sgd. Rev. G. J. Dobson.*'

Webb straightened. He was sure, now, that what he suspected was true, and a leaden weight had settled in his stomach. He thanked the caretaker and, taking Sheila's arm, hurried her down the path. But almost at once she pulled back, bringing him to a halt.

'Just a minute, David: I'd like to look at Mum and Dad's graves while we're here.'

Intent on pursuing his inquiries, Webb hesitated, irritated at the delay and ashamed of being so. Taking his assent for granted, Sheila had already branched off to the left, threading her way over the wet grass in the direction of two silver birches which were casting their shadows over a couple of graves at their feet.

Webb had attended the funerals of both his parents, but had visited neither grave since. Now, following his sister, he joined her as she stood looking down at the neatly kept plots and the summer flowers which grew there. And was aware of much the same feelings he'd experienced when they were alive—for his mother affection tempered with impatience, for his father exasperated resentment. Now, though, this latter was allied with a more immediate frustration. Even from the grave, Webb thought helplessly, his father was impeding his progress, muddying decisions which should have been clear-cut and unambiguous.

Sheila gave a small sigh and turned away, and he fell into step beside her, glad to leave behind his uncomfortable memories. Unconsciously his steps quickened and she gave a little skip to keep up with him.

'David, is the fact that it was Joan Wainwright's grave significant?'

'No,' he answered grimly, 'that's just an ironic twist. What matters is that the grave was filled in on the day Dick disappeared.'

She frowned. 'I don't understand.'

'I've a feeling, Sheila, that Dick never left Erlesborough, and that what you saw that night was his murderer taking advantage of the new grave to bury his body on top of his sister's. What's more,' he added, opening the gate for her, 'I think that Billy Makepeace arrived at the same conclusion.'

CHAPTER 7

Chief Superintendent Phil Fleming sat behind his desk gazing into space and tugging at his lower lip. After a while he turned back to his subordinate.

'It's an extraordinary conclusion to jump to, Spider, and I'm blessed if I follow your reasoning. As a child your sister thought she saw a ghost, and on the basis of that, God knows how many years later, you want to dig up the grave of a respectable citizen because there might—only might, mark you—be an extra body in there with her. Surely you see how thin it is?'

Webb said heavily, 'It fits too well to be coincidence, sir.' He paused. 'If you remember, I mentioned at the start of the case that I knew the people concerned. You asked me to go ahead, but the deeper I get into it, the more personally I seem to be involved. In the circumstances, I wonder if you might reconsider? I'd be much happier handing over to DI Crombie. He's a competent officer and—'

'Don't sing Crombie's praises to me, Chief Inspector,' Fleming cut in sharply, 'I'm well aware of them. But as I said at the outset, you're uniquely placed in this case, and it's no time to be squeamish. Good God, man, you must have come across cases before that you're less than comfortable with, but that's no reason to throw your hand in.' He paused, eyeing Webb with his head on one side in what the Chief Inspector thought of as his sparrow mode.

'Mind you, should a genuine conflict of interest develop you can see me again, but having requested an exhumation order you must at least see that through.'

Webb relaxed slightly. So he had got his way on that point.

'Which,' Fleming continued, pulling his phone towards him, 'you will appreciate is a vote of confidence in your assessment of the situation. I hope I don't regret it.'

*

Once put in motion, the formalities were completed quickly and after an early lunch Webb and Jackson returned to Erlesborough, the Coroner's Warrant for Exhumation in Webb's pocket.

'We'll call in and see the vicar first,' he said, as they approached the outskirts of the town. 'Old Dobson, of course, is long dead.'

But though the incumbent had changed several times since Webb's boyhood, the vicarage of St Gabriel's, on the opposite side of the church to the school, looked exactly as he remembered it, a steeply gabled house in Cotswold stone. A child's tricycle was abandoned on the lawn. He pushed open the gate and walked up the path, Jackson at his heels.

The woman who opened the door was in her thirties, and a small boy—no doubt the owner of the trike—clung to her skirt.

'DCI Webb, ma'am, Shillingham CID. Is the vicar at home? I'm afraid I don't know his name?'

'Morris, Ted Morris. Yes, he's working on his sermon. Is it about Mr Makepeace?' she added, as they stepped into the hall.

'In a way,' Webb said vaguely.

The Reverend Ted Morris looked disconcertingly young to Webb as he rose from his desk and came forward holding out his hand. Obviously his mental image of parsons was out of date.

'Yes, Chief Inspector: how can I help you?'

'I'm afraid, sir, we have a rather distressing duty to perform.' He extracted the warrant from his pocket and handed it over.

The vicar read it, his brow creasing. 'Dear me. I haven't been involved in an exhumation before, but I suppose we can be thankful it's not a recent burial.'

Which sentiment Jackson silently endorsed, though as much for the sake of the diggers as of the deceased's family.

Morris handed back the document. 'I don't see the

connection, though. Surely you're working on Mr Make-peace's death?'

Webb smiled. 'The police, like the Almighty, work in mysterious ways. But yes, I'd be grateful for anything you can tell me about him. You'd have known him well?'

Despairing of an early return to his sermon, Ted Morris waved him to a chair. 'He was my Vicar's Warden. When I first came to the parish he was extremely kind, both to me and my wife. I'll always be grateful for that.'

'Was he a popular man, would you say?'

Morris considered. 'Not exactly popular. Respected, yes, but he'd a sharp tongue and was inclined to be opinionated. He occasionally got people's backs up.'

'Were you aware of any more serious ill-feeling?'

'I believe there was some feud he'd been involved in, but the other man died shortly before I came here. Nothing else, as far as I know.'

'Then was he particularly friendly with anyone?'

The vicar shrugged. 'He belonged to the Farmers' Club, but I don't know who he met there. And I believe Gus Lang, our organist, had an occasional drink with him.'

Tom Vernon had mentioned that. It would be worth following up.

'Could you give us the names and addresses of those he came into contact with at the church—sidesmen and so on?'

The vicar rose, detached a sheet of paper from a notice-board hanging on his wall, and handed it to Webb. It was a list of church officials, giving addresses and phone numbers. Webb nodded his thanks and passed it to Jackson.

'You can keep it,' Morris said, as the sergeant resignedly began to copy out the names, 'I'll get another.'

'Thank you.' Webb moved from the general to the particular. 'Mr Morris, were you at home on Monday evening?'

'No, I was taking a confirmation class.'

'And your wife?'

Morris looked surprised. 'She was in, yes.'

'Did she take any phone-calls for you?'

Morris smiled ruefully. 'There are always phone-calls, Chief Inspector.'

'Can you remember offhand who they were from?'

'Some, yes. Billy Makepeace, for one. I was sorry to have missed him, especially in the circumstances.'

Webb let his breath out in a long sigh. 'What time would that have been?'

'I'm not sure. Just a minute, I'll ask my wife.' He went to the door, opened it and called 'Val!' and, as his wife appeared, 'Can you remember what time Billy phoned on Monday?'

'It was while I was bathing Luke. About a quarter to eight.'

Immediately, no doubt, after he'd tried Sheila.

'He didn't leave a message, Mrs Morris? Ask your husband to phone back, or anything?'

'No, though he sounded put out Ted wasn't here. And he didn't put the phone down immediately; it was as if he was wondering what to do. Then he just said, "All right, Val, thanks," and hung up.'

There was a crash and a yell in the distance, and with a muttered apology she hurried away.

'About the exhumation,' her husband said, 'when will it take place?'

'Four o'clock tomorrow morning.' Seeing the man's eyes widen, Webb added, 'We try to arrange it before it gets light and there are people about. You don't have to be there yourself, sir. The superintendent of the cemetery will attend, and various police officers, though if you'd like to come you will, of course, be welcome.'

Ted Morris bit his lip. 'I think perhaps I'll give it a miss,' he said. 'It's not as though I knew Mrs Wainwright personally.'

Webb nodded. 'Is her husband still alive, do you know?'

'Would that be Sam Wainwright, of Lansdown Road?'

'That's the one.'

'I'm sorry, I hadn't made the connection. I didn't know he'd been married before. Yes, Sam's still alive. He's not a regular worshipper, but he puts in an appearance at Christmas and Easter.' He paused. 'Did his first wife die young?'

'Thirty-eight.'

He shook his head sadly. 'And there's some doubt about the cause? A bit belated, isn't it?'

Webb had no intention of revealing his real interest in the grave. 'Things sometimes crop up years later,' he said evasively.

'Well, I hope you'll go easy on him; he's an elderly man, you know.'

'We'll break it as gently as we can.' Webb stood up. 'Thanks for your help, Mr Morris.' He glanced at the open reference books on the desk. 'I hope we didn't drive away your muse.'

'Joan's grave?' Sam Wainwright repeated unbelievingly. 'But . . . why?'

'We want to satisfy ourselves there's no irregularity,' Webb said soothingly.

'What does irregularity matter, after all this time? Leave her be.'

'Mr Wainwright, we wouldn't be doing this if we hadn't good reason. I promise you that as soon as we've satisfied ourselves she'll be buried again with all due reverence, and everything will be as before.'

The old man looked at him shrewdly. 'You're young Davy Webb, aren't you? I heard from my nephews you were sniffing around.'

'Now, Sam,' said his wife, glancing at Webb apologetically. She was a large woman in her seventies, with a pleasant face and homely manner. Webb reckoned Sam's second marriage had been a happy one. He turned to her.

'Did you know the first Mrs Wainwright, ma'am?'

She flushed to find herself the centre of attention. 'Not well, but I'd met her. My first husband was killed in the war, leaving me with two little girls. When we met in the

street, Mrs Wainwright—' she said the name diffidently—
'made a fuss of them, not having any of her own.' She smiled
reminiscently. 'Funny to think they're both grandmothers
now.'

Her husband moved impatiently. 'It's Makepeace's
death that concerns you, Webb.'

'Yes indeed,' Webb said easily, glad of the lead-in. 'Were
you involved in the family feud, sir?'

The old man made a sound of disgust. 'No, I didn't
hold with it—grown men behaving like fools. I told Dick
straight, he could leave me out of it.'

'So you were on friendly terms with Mr Makepeace?'

'I'd not exactly say friendly, but we passed the time of
day.'

'Where were you on Monday evening, sir?' Webb asked
innocently.

'Monday? That was our whist night. We play every fort-
night.' He stirred, remembering the purpose of the visit.
'Anyway, like I said, you find who killed old Makepeace
and leave us alone. No call that I can see to go digging up
respectable folks that died long since.'

His wife put her plump, speckled hand over his. 'They'll
treat her right, love, never you fret. She won't come to any
harm.'

The old man was silent, staring down at the carpet with
rheumy eyes, the unexpected visit bringing back to mind
the woman he had loved and lost half a lifetime ago.

Webb stood up, nodding to Jackson. 'We'll let you know
when everything's over,' he said.

'Will you need me at the exhumation, Guv?' Jackson
inquired diffidently.

'No, Ken, you get your night's sleep. I'll stay at my
sister's again. Did you get on to the undertakers?'

'Yep. Same firm, so there should be no problem about
identifying the coffin. All this fuss,' he added, 'and it's not
even the woman we're interested in.'

'We have to play it by the book.'

'Let's just hope you're right, and the bloke is in there with her.' Otherwise, he thought to himself, there'll be hell to pay, from the relatives if not the Chief Super.

Webb made no comment. His own thoughts, as so often in this case, were ambivalent. A second body would vindicate his request for exhumation; on the other hand, its discovery would be what, at a subconscious level, he had been dreading for the last forty years. And instead of investigating one death, which was proving sticky enough, he would be called on to solve two.

Rousing himself from his brooding, he said, 'Pass that church list to Dawson at the briefing, Ken. He and Cummings can make a start on it tomorrow. Cross off the organist, though, I'll see him myself. What we want is people's reactions to Makepeace, a note of anyone he's known to have upset recently—in fact, anything that might be of interest. General gossip, really.'

He glanced at his watch. 'And talking of the briefing, it's time we were on our way there.'

They arrived at Silver Street to find Larry Vernon pacing the lobby.

'What the hell's going on?' he burst out, as Webb came through the swing-doors. 'I hear you've been to my uncle with some wild story of digging up Aunt Joan.'

Aware of turning heads, Webb took his elbow and steered him firmly towards an interview room. 'Please, Mr Vernon, keep your voice down. We don't want the whole town to know about it.'

'I'll bet you don't! I never heard of such a crackpot idea! God, do you know how long she's been dead?'

'To the day. And also that your father disappeared the day after her funeral.'

'Meaning what?' demanded Vernon belligerently. 'You can hardly blame her for that!'

'Have you told your mother about the disinterment?' Webb asked quietly.

Vernon looked at him suspiciously. 'Not yet. I phoned her, but she was out.'

'It might be kinder to wait till it's over. It wouldn't be very pleasant for her to lie awake thinking of her sister-in-law's grave being opened.' Even if she didn't realize it was her husband's body they were looking for.

Larry Vernon opened his mouth, presumably to assert his right to tell his mother anything he chose. Then, belatedly, he saw the sense of Webb's words, and nodded grudgingly. 'You could be right.'

'Good,' Webb said pleasantly. 'Your uncle will, of course, be given a full report of our findings.'

'I can't think what started you on this wild-goose chase,' Vernon began again. 'I'd have thought you'd got your work cut out tracking down Makepeace's killer without bothering with someone who's been dead for years.'

'I'll explain later,' Webb said, 'but you'll have to excuse me now; I'm due at a meeting upstairs.'

And before Larry Vernon had the chance to say more, he was shepherded politely but firmly out of the door.

After the briefing, having checked with Sheila that he could again spend the night at The Old Farmhouse, Webb called on the church organist, Gus Lang.

The man who opened the door to them was in his late sixties, tall and with a military bearing. He looked vaguely familiar, and when Webb identified himself a small smile touched his lips under the bristly moustache.

'Come in,' he said, adding as they complied, 'You don't remember me, do you?'

He had shown them into a pleasantly shabby room with a piano in one corner, and it was that which gave Webb his clue.

'Mr Lang—of course. You taught music at St Gabriel's.' As he spoke, he recalled the dark young man whose patience he had tried more than once.

'That's right. I remember you as a small boy who used to sit at the back of the class, drawing throughout the lesson. I confiscated several of your artistic efforts, among them a very creditable cartoon of myself.'

Webb smiled. 'I remember.'

Jackson wondered if the man realized that the acclaimed cartoons which spasmodically appeared in the *Broadshire News* came from the same source. Possibly not, since they were signed enigmatically with an S in a circle—a spider in a web.

'You're here about Makepeace, of course,' Lang said, seating himself in a deep winged chair. 'A curmudgeonly old devil, but I liked him. It's a shocking thing to have happened.'

'I believe you used to meet occasionally outside the church?'

'Yes, we'd have a pint together now and then.' Lang steepled his long fingers and regarded them thoughtfully. 'I knew your father, too. Played bowls with him quite regularly until he became ill. I tried once to bring him and Billy together, but they rounded on me with equal ferocity and I had to give up.'

'It was a stupid business,' Webb said, aware of Jackson's interest. 'Do you remember Dick Vernon, sir?'

Lang looked surprised at what appeared to him to be a change of subject. 'Only vaguely,' he replied. 'He disappeared soon after I came to Erlesborough.'

Webb returned to his original topic. 'Was Makepeace at odds with anyone else?'

Lang gave a short laugh. 'Frequently. He didn't suffer fools gladly, and in his opinion there were a lot of them about.'

'Hardly the attitude of a churchman,' Webb commented.

'Make no mistake about it, Chief Inspector, Billy was a good man. His heart was in the right place even if he was tetchy, and if anyone was in trouble he'd move heaven and earth to help them. As regards your father,' he added, sensing Webb's scepticism, 'it was six of one and half a dozen of the other. Lord knows what they fell out about all those years ago, but neither of them was prepared to forget it.'

Which was not the impression Mrs Makepeace had

given. It seemed Billy had not admitted his wish for recon-
ciliation, probably in case John Webb turned it down.

'Did he discuss his farm with you?'

'*Ad nauseam!*'

'What was his opinion of his manager?'

Lang shrugged. 'Typically, Billy felt he'd be better off
without him. In fact he considered getting rid of him, but
I talked him out of it. With his heart condition, he wouldn't
have lasted a month on his own.'

Webb wondered whether Croft had been aware of these
deliberations. 'What had Makepeace got against him?'

'Mainly that he was young and full of new ideas which,
according to Billy, would cost a fortune to implement. He
was always grumbling that Croft didn't know the value of
money. The man was in personal difficulties, too; Billie'd
had to bale him out with a loan. Mind you, I bet he charged
a good rate of interest!'

The ironic smile was back again. 'It's a perfect example
of Billy's philosophy: he'd never refuse help, but if he considered people had brought on their own misfortunes, he
couldn't resist teaching them a lesson at the same time.'

'What'll happen to the loan now?' Webb wondered
aloud.

'I've no idea. The chap's probably on tenterhooks.'

Jerry Croft would warrant another visit. He'd call there
before he went to Sheila's.

'Mr Makepeace was on the Bench, wasn't he?' Webb
said reflectively. It could well be that some villain had taken
exception to Billy's philosophy.

Lang's sharp glance showed that he'd followed Webb's
reasoning. 'He was, yes, but you'd need to speak to the
other magistrates about that.'

'I'll do that.' Webb got to his feet. 'Incidentally, sir,
where were you on Monday evening?'

'Bell-ringing practice, after which we repaired to the
Crown as usual. But I was home by eleven.'

Webb nodded. 'Well, thanks for your help. And despite
my endless doodling,' he added with a smile, 'you managed

to instil a love of music into me which has given me a great deal of pleasure over the years. I'm very grateful.'

Jerry Croft closed the stable door and wiped his forehead with the back of his hand. It was six o'clock, and he was ready for a shower and a glass of cold beer. He glanced uncertainly at the farmhouse, but there was no sign of life. Still, Sally would have checked on the old lady on her return from school. And Mrs Hawthorn would be back soon; she was staying here at the moment, though, with the tourist season in full swing, she'd been unable to take time off work.

Lord, what a mess it all was! He knew Sally was as much on edge as he was with all the uncertainty; knew, too, that if they had to move out of the area there'd be all the fuss about her job having to be the one that was sacrificed.

But damn it, what was he supposed to do? He couldn't just kick his heels because she and the kids were nicely settled at St Gay's. More serious was the fact that if they *did* have to move, it would mean repaying the loan. The old woman couldn't be expected to continue it once they were out of her employ. And where, Croft wondered despairingly, would he find another employer willing to take it on? For all his faults, old Makepeace had had his good points.

Suppose, he thought, his heart plummeting still further, they had to remove Mother from the nursing home? There was no place for her under the National Health; his frantic inquiries had been met with the implicit suggestion that he should take her into his own home. But how could he, when she was wandering like that? There was no one in the house all day, and she couldn't be left alone. Not to mention the effect it would have on the kids.

He had reached the gate in the hedge when the sound of a car drawing up made him pause. Then, as Webb got out of it, he felt a wave of impotent anger. Another grilling was the last thing he needed.

'Good afternoon, Mr Croft,' Webb was saying over the five-barred gate. 'I'm glad I caught you.'

The red-headed sergeant wasn't with him; perhaps this was an informal visit—or intended to seem so.

Croft said ungraciously, 'More questions?'

'A few, I'm afraid. I shan't keep you long.'

'Go in next door, then, and I'll see you there.'

Webb nodded pleasantly and strolled along the pavement, and with a sigh Croft went through the gate to his own property. The children were playing a skipping game in the drive, hair flying and brown legs flashing as they kept up the complicated rhythm. Not a care in the world, he thought sourly, and was instantly ashamed of his resentment.

Circumnavigating them, he opened the front door, called to Sally that he was home, and led Webb into the farm office where they'd spoken before. The shower and the beer would have to wait.

'You'll appreciate we're having to look very closely into Mr Makepeace's affairs,' Webb began, seating himself in the chair he'd occupied on his last visit, 'and there's been mention of a loan you received. Could you give me some details?'

'My God, it didn't take you long.' Croft sat down heavily in the desk chair. 'It was a personal matter, nothing to do with the farm.'

'So I understand,' Webb said, and waited politely. Croft ran a hand through his hair.

'If you must know, we've had to put my mother in a private nursing home. Not from choice, but because it was the only one to have room for her. She has Alzheimer's. I can't afford the fees and we've not enough security for a bank loan, so Mr Makepeace agreed to step in. It was all quite legit, interest accruing and so on.'

So Lang had misjudged him; this misfortune was not self-induced. 'How much was the loan for?'

Croft named what seemed to Webb an extortionate figure, but then, thank God, he knew nothing of nursing-home costs.

'We're paying it off every month,' Croft said quickly, aware of his surprise.

'Did you get on well with your employer?'

The man seemed glad of the shift to business matters. 'On the whole, though we clashed once or twice. I was keen to introduce new methods, but he wouldn't hear of them.'

'Will Mrs Makepeace be staying on here?'

Croft shrugged. 'She's been here fifty years, I shouldn't think she'd want to leave. Unless she goes into a home, too,' he added bitterly. 'Her daughter lives in town, but she's out at her job, so the old girl wouldn't be much better off there.'

'I asked you before if you knew of any disagreements Makepeace might have been involved in. Have you remembered anything in the interval?'

'No. If you ask me, your best bet would be to follow up his cases in Court. They get a rough element up before them.'

'Thank you, yes, that's being looked into. Well,' he rose to his feet, 'I won't keep you any longer. And I hope your family worries sort themselves out.'

Croft, surprised at the human touch, nodded and showed him to the door. Amen to that, he thought devoutly.

CHAPTER 8

Webb drove slowly the few hundred yards to his sister's home, turning over in his mind what he had heard. Suppose, contrary to the impression he'd been given, old Makepeace had tried to call in the loan for some reason? Croft was near to breaking-point, that much was obvious. Any such move could have panicked him into action, temporarily blinding him to the fact that Billy was more use to him alive than dead.

Tentatively, eyes on the road ahead, Webb cast Croft in the rôle of murderer. The man was a tightly coiled spring of repression, competent enough but continually frustrated in his job—and possibly in his marriage too. It might be illuminating to see man and wife together.

He had reached The Old Farmhouse gateway and, seeing the dog come gambolling up to greet him, Webb shrugged off his introspection. He'd defer any further speculation until he knew what the night's digging would unearth.

After supper the family again separated, Stephen to his postponed game of tennis, Lyn to study, Colin to the local Horticultural Society. Sheila had intended accompanying him, and Webb urged her not to stay home on his account; but she insisted she had a headache and was glad of the excuse not to go.

'Friday's always hectic,' she said. 'I get up an hour early to start baking, and I'm usually exhausted by the end of it.'

They settled by the window with their coffee and Webb felt a momentary qualm. It was many years since they'd been alone together for any length of time; suppose they found nothing to talk about?

'I saw Jenny again yesterday,' he remarked to open the conversation. 'We were talking about the split between Billy and the others. Did you ever hear what happened?'

'No—no, I didn't.'

Webb repeated the story of the party and the high-spirited young men in the car. She listened in silence, then sighed, shaking her head.

'What a tragedy. I never knew Billy had been an athlete.'

'Nor I. But that's only half the story; what surprised me was that Father and Dick, though not particularly friendly, remained on speaking terms for several more years. She didn't know what caused that rift.'

Sheila was gazing out of the window, and something in her face made him say sharply, 'Do you?'

She avoided his eyes, lifting one hand in a helpless little gesture.

'Well, Sheila? Do you?'

She said slowly, 'Yes, as it happens I do; Mum told me just before she died. But I had to promise not to tell anyone.'

Webb said harshly, 'I'm not "anyone", I'm her son.'

'And a policeman to boot. Which means if tonight goes as expected, Dick's background will be investigated anyway.'

Tonight. What would he know that he'd prefer not to, before it was over? If Dick's body really were in Joan's grave, it could mean the confirmation of everything he dreaded. God, he thought suddenly, what was he thinking of, going through with this? The exhumation was entirely his doing; he'd had no need to apply for it. But, as Sheila remarked, he was a policeman, and a conviction had been growing in him that Billy's death and Dick's disappearance were linked. So, after all, he had had no choice.

He looked up, meeting his sister's concerned eyes.

'Go on, then,' he said.

'The row was over Mum.'

He tensed, instinctively rejecting her words, concentrating instead on the soft upholstery under his hand, the shadows striking across the garden, the steady breathing of the dog at his feet. Then, despite himself, they filtered through to understanding and acceptance.

When he made no comment, Sheila went on: 'She was engaged to Dick, you see, but Dad, who hadn't shown any interest in her before, suddenly muscled in.' Her voice shook. 'I don't think he loved her, David. I think it was just a way to score off Dick—the old, bloody rivalry again.'

There was silence. It fitted, Webb thought dully. He wondered he'd not thought of it before.

'And I also think—though she didn't say so—that she never completely stopped loving Dick, nor he her.'

It was a novelty, this picture of his mother as tragic heroine. He remembered her as weak, discontented, showing little affection to either husband or children. Had his father been happy with his prize? Or—and Webb saw this in a flash of insight—having won her, was he bitterly disillusioned—by her peevishness, her lack of interest, her general spinelessness?

And how must his mother have felt? To a young girl, two men fighting over her must have seemed the essence of romance, straight out of the pulp fiction she read so avidly. How, then, would she react when she realized she'd deserted the man she loved for a taciturn, stubborn character who, at least in his son's hearing, never gave her so much as a word of endearment? After all these years, Webb understood what lay behind the tragedy of his parents' marriage—corrosive resentment at the hand fate had dealt them.

Sheila was staring out of the window, twisting a handkerchief in her hands. He said, 'There's more, isn't there?'

She nodded. 'Something she let slip. We'd been talking about Dick and wondering where he could have got to, and Mum suddenly said, "The odd thing is, I saw him that night, and he never mentioned leaving." And then she looked frightened, and I couldn't get any more out of her.'

Yet another facet to the night when he'd hidden in the barn and Sheila set out to find her teddy-bear.

'I've been thinking about it ever since I got back from the cemetery,' she continued. 'The dates tied in; it would have been the day after Joan's funeral. Dick must have been shattered, specially since she was his twin. Perhaps he turned to Mum for a bit of comfort.'

'Wouldn't that be his wife's province?' Webb asked, and saw her eyebrows lift at the harshness in his voice.

'I heard she and Joan never got on. Probably jealous of each other.'

They sat in silence, engrossed in their own thoughts, and Webb, glancing suddenly at his sister, experienced a jolt. For a fleeting moment in the half-light it could have been his mother sitting there: the same profile with its rounded cheek, the same softly curling hair. Then the door opened and Lyn's voice said cheerfully, 'In the gloaming?' The room flooded with light and the resemblance fled, restoring Sheila to her competent, practical self.

'I've come down for more coffee,' Lyn was saying. 'Would you like some?'

Sheila smiled at her. 'Thanks, darling.'

As she went out, Webb said suddenly, 'Did you tell anyone about Billy phoning you?'

'Outside the family, you mean? I don't think so. Why?'

'It would be as well not to mention it, nor what you and the others were talking about in the café.' Though from what he'd seen of Janet Conway, he imagined that story had already been passed round.

Before she could comment, Lyn returned and handed each of them a mug of steaming coffee. She was barefoot as usual, and wearing what looked like one of Colin's old shirts outside her jeans. Whatever happened to glamour? Webb wondered as she padded out of the room.

Sheila looked after her fondly. 'Susan thinks the world of her, you know.'

'*Susan?*' It was so long since Webb had thought of his ex-wife that for a moment he wasn't sure who Sheila was referring to.

'Yes; she never forgets her birthday. I've always felt she'd have liked children of her own.'

This unsuspected view of his wife following swiftly on the revelation about his mother roused Webb to irritable self-defence.

'If so, it's the first I've heard of it.'

Sheila said quickly, 'Oh, I didn't mean to imply—' and broke off, uncertain how to continue. He didn't help her. The gulf between them was still there, he thought sadly. Though it could be temporarily bridged, basically they were doomed to stand one on each side of it, staring helplessly across at each other. But then they'd never been a family unit, simply four separate individuals, forced by circumstance to live under the same roof.

'What time will you have to get up?' Sheila asked.

'Three-thirty; I'll set the clock-radio. Actually, Sheila, if you don't mind I won't wait up for Colin. I'd like to get in as many hours' sleep as possible before everything gets going again.'

'Of course.'

Aware of the lingering constraint between them, he said awkwardly, 'I do appreciate it, your putting me up. I'd hardly have had any sleep otherwise.'

'You know you're welcome,' she said.

The graveyard lay silent in the pre-dawn hush, the only sound the rhythmic thudding of spades hitting the clogged earth. The air was chill, and a heavy dew covered the grass. Screens, unnecessary at the moment, had been erected against later sightseers, and arc lamps created a small, brilliantly lit oasis.

On the fringe of it a group of men huddled together in atavistic comradeship, the living among the dead; though in fact death was no stranger to any of them. They included the superintendent of the cemetery, Dr Stapleton the pathologist, Fred Furlong from the undertakers, a police photographer and half a dozen constables who were taking turns in the digging.

'Go carefully,' Webb had instructed them. 'What we're looking for is an extra body dumped on top of the coffin, but we don't know at what depth it might be. When you get down a couple of feet—carefully, mind—I want you to abandon the spades and use trowels. We can't risk damaging any evidence.'

The Broadshire soil was light and loamy and once the turf had been removed the work was not too strenuous. Large plastic sheets had been spread on the ground to receive all the earth removed from the grave, and two men were engaged in sifting the spadesful as they fell. The sky was fading to a soft turquoise, and already pink and gold strands were appearing to the east where the sun would shortly rise.

Furlong the undertaker had lit a cigarette and a spiral of pungent smoke drifted over them, marring, to Webb's mind, the freshness of the morning. To escape it, he moved a few feet to one side. And suddenly a vivid memory, long forgotten, flooded his mind: a picture of his father sitting across the hearth in the Lower Road house, eyes narrowed against the smoke and ash falling from the cigarette in his thick, nicotine-stained fingers. Here, in this chilly cemetery forty years on, Webb realized for the first time that his lifelong dislike of smoking dated from that buried memory.

Consigning it back into the past, he glanced at the screen that hid the open grave. Surely if anything was there they'd have found it by now? He was torn between the hope that they'd reach the coffin without incident, and the need to vindicate this exercise. If it proved a wild-goose chase, Dick's disappearance and Sheila's ghost would both remain a mystery.

Then, cutting into his thoughts, Pike's voice reached him, raised in excitement. 'Guv, we've found something!'

Webb hurried forward, his ambivalence forgotten. 'Well done, lads. What is it?' He peered into the dank, damp hole as Pike eagerly pointed out their find—a piece of bone shining obscenely under the arc lamps. Webb stared at it for a long minute, buffeted by conflicting emotions. 'Right, then,' he said. 'Easy does it, now. See if you can ease him out in one piece.'

The digging continued for another hour, more specialized now and requiring infinite patience, recorded systematically by the flashing camera. From time to time the tedium was relieved by lesser triumphs as the constables sifting the soil came upon first three shirt buttons then, minutes later, a tarnished metal watch.

Those not immediately involved had withdrawn slightly, splitting naturally into twos and threes as they sipped hot coffee and watched the sun rise. Over to their left a cock was crowing; the day was about to begin. Webb turned as Tenby, who had been taking his turn with the excavation, approached him.

'We've struck a problem, Guv. The lid of the coffin's caved in at some stage and our lad seems to have fallen through, along with half a ton of earth. What we first saw was his foot sticking up, but it's going to be the devil of a job sorting out t'other from which.'

Webb felt his stomach turn. 'They're jumbled together?'

'Depends how intact they are—we can't tell yet because of the soil. The clothes will have disintegrated long since, so there'll be no help from that quarter.'

'You are sure there are two bodies?' Webb demanded urgently. 'That bone can't have come from inside the coffin?'

'No, the angle's not right. The skeleton we can see was never in the coffin. Not intentionally, that is.'

'Then we'll have to remove the whole lot together. Get the ropes in position, would you?'

He stood watching with the other men while the gruesome work progressed. 'Do you reckon my theory holds water,' he asked Stapleton, 'and they were buried within a day or two of each other?'

The pathologist lifted thin shoulders. 'Since both are skeletons, I can't possibly say until we've run tests.'

Stiff-necked bastard! Webb thought in a wave of frustrated impatience; he might have known Stapleton wouldn't give him anything. But the pathologist relented slightly. 'Trouble is, all the small bones will have fallen together into the bottom of the coffin—wrist bones, fingers and so on. It'll take time to separate and label them.'

'I wonder what chance there is of tracing Vernon's dental records,' Webb mused. 'They'd be the quickest means of identification.'

Stapleton gave a thin-lipped smile. 'At least you seem in no doubt who we have here, Chief Inspector,' he said drily.

By the time the mortuary van left and the earth and turf from the grave had been parcelled up and despatched to the laboratory, it was almost lunch-time.

The cemetery had been opened as usual but the screens remained, with a couple of uniformed constables on duty to keep sightseers at bay. The small crowd which had gathered as news of the operation spread, dispersed once the shrouded coffin had been removed, and apart from an occasional slowly moving car whose driver craned to see what was happening, Chapel Lane had reverted to its normal quietness.

Since both the deceased had presumably been dead forty-odd years, there was not the usual urgency about post-mortems. They had therefore been fixed for the Monday morning to allow time for removal of the soil and preliminary sorting out of the two bodies. Webb did not regret the postponement.

Jackson, who'd arrived shortly before nine o'clock, ambled over to the gate where Webb was briefing the SOCO photographer and waited till the man got into his car and set off back to Shillingham. 'Right, Guv, what's next on the agenda?'

'I want to check with Silver Street who handled Vernon's disappearance.'

'He won't still be around, surely?'

'Someone might be. Anyway, we need to read up the notes and see if anything significant comes to light. First, though,' he added, 'I could do with a good wash, a cold beer and a plate of ham sandwiches.'

'All available at the Narrow Boat,' Jackson suggested with a grin.

'You talked me into it,' Webb said.

In Silver Street, representatives of the Press had taken up position outside the police station, among whom Webb recognized Bill Hardy, crime reporter of the *Broadshire News*. He and Jackson shouldered their way through, holding the pack at bay with promises of a Press conference later in the day.

In his upstairs office, Inspector Charlton was also eager for their news.

'Well, how did it go? Did you find what you were looking for?'

'It seems so,' Webb said a touch wearily.

'You mean there really *were* two bodies in the grave?'

'There were indeed.'

'And it's that man who disappeared yonks ago?'

'Seems likely.'

Charlton considered for a moment. 'What I don't understand, sir, is what put you on to it? Does it tie in with the
Makepeace case?'

Webb was loath to embark on Sheila's ghost story, but
the man deserved some explanation. 'Basically, I believe
Makepeace overheard something which made him suspect
what had happened. We know that before he set off for the
Farmers' Club he tried to phone the vicar, who was out.
We also know he was late arriving at the club, which could
indicate that he called on someone on the way.'

'And confided his suspicions?'

'That's the most likely explanation.'

'And it was the wrong person to confide in?'

'Almost certainly. My guess is that whoever it was
pressed secrecy on him, let him go on to the club while he
decided what to do, and then lay in wait for him on his way
home.'

'And have you any idea who this might be, sir?'

Webb sighed. 'Regrettably, not a clue. But leaving Makepeace for the moment, Inspector, I need the files on Vernon's disappearance. I presume they're at HQ?'

'Bound to be, sir. I've never come across them here,
though the case is still talked about. George Harvey was in
charge; he might be able to help you.'

Webb brightened. 'He's still around?'

'Very much so. Bit creaky in the joints, but a great old
feller. Must be eighty if he's a day, but his memory's still
sound, especially on the Vernon case. It was his one regret
when he retired that he'd never been able to tie it up.'

'Could we make an appointment to see him?'

'Certainly, I'll do it now. When would you like to go?'

'As soon as convenient.'

They waited while Charlton put through the call and,
without going into details, relaid their request.

'Three o'clock?' he repeated, raising his eyebrows at

Webb, who nodded. 'Right, Guv, they'll be along then. Cheers.

'He and his missus live in sheltered accommodation,' Charlton went on as he replaced the phone. 'Glebe Court, it is, just up the hill from St Gabriel's.'

'Thanks very much, Inspector, we'll find it. Now, how many dental practices are there in town?'

'Let's see: four that I can think of.'

'Old-established, or new?'

'I'd say they've all changed hands over the years. There was a lot of upheaval over National Health charges and so on. Lake and Gregson in Bridge Street take only private patients now.'

'Could you arrange for a back-up team to visit them all, with a view to tracing Dick Vernon's records?'

The Inspector looked dubious. 'I'll send them, certainly, but it's asking rather a lot after—what?—forty years?'

With which Webb had gloomily to agree.

The day whose clear dawn he had witnessed from the cemetery had clouded over, trapping the hot air with claustrophobic heaviness. The shoppers on the pavements moved slowly, fractious children dragging on their mothers' hands. As they rounded the corner by the vicarage, Webb caught sight of the child Luke in the garden. In the four days of the investigation, he reflected, it was surprising what a wide sweep of the community had been involved in his questions. As yet, none of them had provided the right answers.

An old man was waiting for them as they turned into Glebe Court—doubtless ex-DCI George Harvey. He came forward eagerly as Webb extracted himself from the car, and held out his hand.

'DCI Webb? A pleasure, my boy. I remember you in short trousers!'

'Please, sir,' Webb protested, 'don't give my sergeant here the impression I've a criminal record!' He introduced Jackson, who also had his hand warmly shaken.

'No, no, I knew you only as John Webb's boy—you and

your little sister. I still see her about the town. Come in, come in.'

He led the way with quiet pride into the spick and span little house from which he'd emerged and where an elderly woman smilingly awaited them. 'My wife, Mildred. I'm sure you could do with a cup of tea and one of Mildred's scones?'

'That sounds very welcome,' Webb answered, knowing that to refuse would upset the old couple, not to mention Jackson, though for himself, his ham sandwiches still sufficed.

The room in which they settled themselves was neat and bright, its window open to the airless afternoon. There was a pipe rack on the mantel, but to Webb's relief the old man did not approach it. For the rest, a scattering of books and magazines, the ubiquitous television, deep easy chairs, made a comfortable environment.

'All on one floor,' Harvey said with satisfaction, 'and alarm bells in every room, should we need them. There are a lot worse places to end one's days.'

'It seems ideal,' Webb said, politically but sincerely.

The requisite small talk over, the old man leant forward, resting his arms on his knees. 'Now, what's this all about? I know you've been working on the Makepeace case, but if you've come to me, it must concern Dick Vernon.'

'That's right, sir, we're told you're the authority on him.'

'Up to a point,' the old man agreed. 'I can tell you everything about him down to the number of teeth he had, but for all that I never fathomed what happened to him.'

'Teeth?' Webb interrupted sharply.

'Yes, lad, teeth. I thought that would interest you. I took the precaution, right at the beginning, of getting a copy of his dental records in case they were needed. You'll find them in the files.'

'God bless you, sir!' Webb said devoutly. 'That's the best news I've had today!'

The old man stared at him. 'You're never saying you *have* found him?'

'Almost definitely.'

Mrs Harvey had returned with a tea-tray complete with lace doilies and paper napkins, and was proceeding to lay out cups and saucers on the low table.

'But—*where*, man? Where the hell was he?'

'In his sister's grave, if we're on the right track.'

'Just fancy!' said Mrs Harvey, handing him a cup of tea.

'Bless my soul!' The old man sat back in his chair, his eyes inward-looking, recalling his own investigations. 'The cemetery. That's about the only place we didn't look for him.'

'Well, there was nothing to indicate he was dead, was there? I gather you had the usual sightings all over the country?'

Harvey brushed that impatiently aside. 'Crank calls, most of them. And he was in there with Joan all the time. His twin sister.' He shook his head, adding with ghoulish relish, 'A shared womb and a shared tomb. Who'd have thought it?'

'Really, George!' Mrs Harvey admonished gently. 'Not at the tea-table, dear!'

'We'll collect the files from HQ when we get back,' Webb went on, biting into a buttery scone and adroitly catching the crumbs on his plate. 'It'll mean going back over it all again, checking everything he did during his last week of life. And what those around him did, too.' He looked across at the old man. 'Did you ever suspect murder, sir?'

'It's always on the cards, with a disappearance like that, but there was damn-all to go on.'

'Any motives emerge?'

'Nary a one. Dick was a popular man, as you'll see from the various testimonies. Mind, I was conscious all along of some holding back.' Harvey shot Webb a look under his bushy grey eyebrows, and he wondered uneasily if the old man was referring to his mother. She was unlikely to have admitted meeting Dick that night.

'And old Makepeace might have known a thing or two,' Harvey was continuing, 'but he's beyond our reach now.'

He paused. 'Are you going to tell me what put you on to the cemetery?'

This time Webb did not dodge the question. As matter-of-factly as he could, he related Sheila's conversation with her friends in the café, Billy's apparent interest, and his subsequent phone-call.

'If Sheila had been in that evening,' he ended heavily, 'Billy might still be alive today.'

George Harvey had listened attentively to the account, his old eyes alert and interested.

'You reckon what your sister saw was the murderer concealing the body?'

'I'm pretty sure of it, but it was quick of Billy to spot it. The key factor would have been Sheila's saying it was forty years ago. Anyway, when he couldn't get hold of her he tried phoning the vicar but he was out, too. According to Mrs Makepeace he made only the two calls, but he might well have visited someone on his way to the club, since he was late getting there.'

'Who could that have been?'

'Presumably,' Webb said wryly, 'someone he thought of as a friend. From the church, perhaps, or a fellow magistrate. I imagine he wanted advice on what he should do.'

'Instead of which he walked straight into the murderer's clutches?'

'That's the only conclusion I can draw.'

Harvey slapped his thigh suddenly, making them all jump. 'By heaven, I wish I was young again! This case was my baby; I'd love to be in at the end of it.'

Webb smiled, draining his cup. 'We might well be glad of your help, sir, since you're so familiar with the background. We'll keep in touch.'

The old man was clearly gratified, and insisted on shaking both their hands again as they left. 'Anything at all I can do,' he assured them, 'just let me know.'

Jackson eased the car out of the courtyard and turned left towards the High Street. 'Where to now, Guv?'

Webb yawned and glanced at his watch. 'Better make it

Silver Street—there's barely half an hour before the Press conference. Once that's over, though, we'll head straight back to Stonebridge. I want to get my hands on those files and extract the dental records for Stapleton. Once we know beyond all doubt we have Dick Vernon, we can really get cracking.'

CHAPTER 9

Force Headquarters was situated in the countryside some ten miles south of Shillingham. There was no village nearby, but an old stone bridge that crossed the river further down the road had given its name to the area.

After signing the requisite forms, Webb and Jackson were escorted down to the basement where the archives were stored and spent some time sifting through the shelves of old and dusty files before they found what they were looking for.

'I'll drive, Ken,' Webb said as, the bulky files under his arm, they walked back to the car. 'I'll drop you off and then look in at the station for a while. Once I've got the dental records off to Stapleton, I want a quick look at these papers to familiarize myself with the case.'

In fact, he worked in his office for a couple of hours, making out his reports and going through the forty-year-old papers with their painstaking details. Not unnaturally, those who had been most systematically questioned after the disappearance were his father and Billy Makepeace, seemingly the only two people in the district with whom Dick Vernon had been on bad terms. Webb read his father's testimony with grim admiration for its deception.

It was only as he found himself nodding off for the second time that he decided to call it a day and go home. He wondered what Hannah was doing.

It was seven o'clock when he reached his flat, and the atmosphere that met him was stale and airless. He poured himself a whisky, then walked from room to room pushing open windows, though the air that came in was still oppressively hot.

Resting his elbows on the windowsill, he stared broodingly down the hill to where the town lay partially hidden under the brownish-yellow haze, periodically sipping his drink as his mind tiredly but obsessively re-ran the past twenty-four hours.

The sound of voices finally roused him as a group of young people came cycling along Hillcrest, tennis racquets strapped to their bikes. He straightened and stretched, aware of the disoriented sensation that comes from lack of sleep. Yet he was still too keyed-up to settle.

Turning to the phone, he dialled Hannah's number, releasing his breath when she lifted her receiver.

'Any chance of a revival course for a spent copper?'

He heard her low laugh. 'Certainly, sir. Day release or residential?'

'Don't tempt me! Seriously, I shan't be very good company; I've been up half the night digging up bodies and I'm on my knees.'

'Then I recommend a lazy supper with music in the background as we watch the sun go down.'

'Since I saw it come up, that sounds most fitting. Bless you. I'll bring a bottle. Half an hour?'

'Fine.'

God, he looked a mess, he thought, catching a glimpse of his reflection in the bathroom mirror. Shadows under the eyes, badly in need of a shave. He bent over the bath and turned the taps on full. Time for a leisurely soak before he went down, but he must be careful not to fall asleep.

By the time he reached Hannah's door he was at least presentable again. 'Third time I've seen you this week,' he commented as he kissed her. 'Hope I'm not pushing my luck.'

She glanced at him, ready with a quick riposte, but something in his face stayed her. 'Of course not,' she amended.

This case was getting to him, she thought, leading the

way to the sitting-room, where an electric fan stirred the sluggish air. He'd been singularly uncommunicative over the drinks on Wednesday, and though she'd read the crime reports in the *News* with more than usual attention, she wasn't much the wiser. An old man he'd known in the past had died—that much he'd told her. It had later turned out to be murder, which was why, no doubt against his will, David had been put on the case. But digging up bodies?

They ate a quiche with one of Hannah's special salads, and the promised music played in the background even if the sun set privately behind its banks of cloud. Conversation was sporadic and Hannah, from long experience, asked no questions, content to wait till he was ready to talk.

There was often a point in his cases when he needed a sounding-board against which to bounce his ideas, to test his theories and voice his doubts. It had to be someone whom he could trust implicitly to respect his confidences, and Hannah was happy to be that person.

That was, in fact, how their relationship had started five years ago, when he'd been dealing with a particularly nasty case of child murder. But such confidences did not come easily to him, and it was usually in the aftermath of their love-making that, lying side by side in the darkness, the torrent of words would suddenly spill out, as though he were no longer capable of withholding them. It might well be that tonight would follow the same pattern.

And so it proved. It was almost a month since they'd been together; they met as friends as frequently as lovers, enjoying each other's company whether or not physical intimacy was involved, and unperturbed when work or other circumstances kept them apart. It was, they felt, an ideal arrangement for two strong-minded individuals, yet there'd been occasions when each had privately acknowledged that their commitment was in fact deeper than they admitted.

That night, though his love-making was as tender and passionate as usual, Hannah was aware of the tension in David, a stress more deep-seated than she'd encountered before. She thought she understood why; this case had

taken him back to the town he'd grown up in and which
he seldom willingly revisited. He'd always been reticent
about his past, and it seemed probable he was now being
forced to face it. She wanted to share it with him, and her
concern was that he mightn't after all feel able to confide
in her.

For a while they lay silently, Hannah afraid to speak lest
she interrupt him on the point of disclosure; and as the
silence lengthened she wondered whether he had fallen
asleep with his problems unrevealed. Then, suddenly, he
reached for her hand and gripped it tightly. Please, she
thought, let me say the right thing; let me help him.

'I'm hating every minute of this case,' he said abruptly.

'So I gathered.'

'It's nearly thirty years since I left Erlesborough, but the
hostility's still there.'

She turned her face to him in a silent question, and flatly,
without embellishment, he told her the story of the family
feud, of Dick Vernon's disappearance and the probable
discovery, that very morning, of his skeleton. Finally, he
related the story of Sheila's ghost, which had drawn his
attention to the cemetery in the first place.

'There's something else, isn't there?' she prompted softly.

'Yes. Ever since Dick disappeared, I've conditioned
myself to believe he was still alive. I daren't *not* believe it.
Subconsciously, I suppose, I was still willing it in the cemetery this morning. Part of me wanted confirmation that
we'd found him, the case cleared up at long last. The other
part dreaded it.'

'But why, darling?'

He began to speak hesitantly, pausing to find the right
words for a story which had remained untold for so long.

'On the day Dick disappeared, one of the boys at school
dared me to go to the old barn that evening and spy on a
courting couple. I accepted the dare and agreed to report
back the next day.

'So, when I was supposed to be in bed, I crept downstairs. My father'd gone out and my mother was in the

kitchen talking to the girl next door. I let myself out of the front door, which we never used and which was kept bolted. I remember moving the bolt only as far along as would release the door, in the hope anyone glancing at it wouldn't realize it was undone.'

He paused and Hannah waited, wondering how this childish escapade could have instigated such long-lasting traumas.

'Well, I made my way to the barn, climbed the outside steps to the hay loft, and as instructed, manœuvred the trapdoor to leave a crack wide enough to give a good view of the barn below. Then I lay down on the hay to wait for the couple to arrive. And, of course, fell asleep.'

He was silent for several long minutes. Then, expressionlessly, he continued. 'I woke to the sound of raised, angry voices, one of which I recognized as my father's. My first thought was that he'd discovered I was missing and somehow known where to find me. I peered through the crack in the floor—the barn door was open and light from the setting sun was streaming through—and to my amazement I saw that the man he was shouting at was Dick Vernon. You can imagine the shock—they hadn't spoken since before I was born. In fact, I was so astonished that at first I didn't take in what they were saying.

'Then my father shouted, ". . . and if there's any more of it, I won't be responsible for the consequences!" And Dick yelled back, "You bloody fool, why don't you *listen*, for God's sake? I *had* to see her, I needed—'; And at that point my father lashed out with his fist, caught Dick on his jaw and sent him crashing to the ground. Then he turned on his heel and stormed out of the barn.

'I lay hardly breathing, waiting for Dick to get up, but he didn't move. I don't know how long I stayed there; it seemed like hours, specially since once the sun had set it got dark quite quickly. I could still make out Dick's figure on the floor, and I got more and more frightened. Eventually I plucked up enough courage to ease myself out of the loft and run home.'

After a pause, which Hannah didn't dare break, he added, 'And by the next evening, everyone was talking about Dick's disappearance. He'd gone out for cigarettes and simply never come back. His car was in the garage, none of his clothes seemed to be missing—he'd simply vanished into thin air. I was probably the last person to see him, but far too terrified to say so. And of course no one thought to ask me. So you see,' he ended heavily, 'why I needed to believe he was alive; if he wasn't, there was a strong possibility my father had killed him.' And he added under his breath, 'Come to that, there still is.'

Hannah said reasonably, 'But if that were so, how did Dick's body get from the barn to the grave?'

She felt him shrug. 'Father could have gone back to check he was OK. After all, he hadn't meant to inflict lasting damage. But if he'd found him dead he might have panicked, remembered Joan's newly dug grave, and—made use of it.'

'On the other hand, it's quite possible Dick came round, set off for home and was run over by a speeding motorist, who then panicked, etcetera, etcetera.'

'If that was the case, the PM will show multiple fractures. It's a possibility, I suppose.'

'You've no idea what they were arguing about?'

David paused, then said heavily, 'I hadn't, until last night. I'd always wondered how the two men had come to be together, when they made a point of avoiding each other. Then Sheila told me she'd found out Mother and Dick Vernon had once been engaged and Mother'd let slip she'd seen him on the night he disappeared. And that explained everything. Dick must have arranged to meet her, and somehow my father got wind of it. She'd probably just left the barn—been summarily dismissed, knowing my father —when their shouting woke me.'

Hannah was silent for a while. Then she said, 'And what of this other man, the one murdered this week? Are the deaths connected?'

'Lord knows; there are endless permutations.'

'Such as?'

'One: perhaps Billy had always suspected Dick was murdered. He overheard Sheila telling her ghost story, put two and two together, and mentioned his suspicions to someone.'

'Who then killed him? At least *that* couldn't have been your father!'

'No, but if Father *had* killed Dick, he might have roped someone else in to help him dispose of the body. Unlikely, I grant you, but possible. And that *might* have been the person Billy went to.' He paused. 'Not very convincing, is it?'

'No. What are the other possibilities?'

'Billy could have killed Dick himself after I left the barn, and the Vernon brothers have just found out. Neither of them has an alibi for the time of the murder.'

'Or?'

'Or Billy's death had nothing to do with Dick's, and it was pure coincidence that he phoned Sheila after overhearing her story. He could just have thought the feud had gone on long enough, as my brother-in-law suggested, and wanted to end it. Mrs Makepeace said as much. In which case, he could have been killed by any of several people whose feathers he'd ruffled.' He was silent, thinking among others of Jerry Croft. Then his thoughts returned to the skeleton. 'But I hope to God the PM shows Vernon died of a stab wound.'

'Even if it was a fractured skull,' Hannah pointed out, 'it didn't necessarily happen in the barn.'

He did not reply.

They lay quietly, side by side in the darkness, and she thought soberly over what he had told her, and also, reading between the lines, what he had not. Of the small boy, starved of affection, haunted for decades by what he'd seen that night; of the man he became, who found it difficult to trust people and whose marriage, possibly affected by that of his parents, had ended in bitterness. And finally of the policeman, disciplined, efficient, whose secret dread was being asked to prove his father's guilt.

She propped herself on one elbow and leaned over to kiss him. 'I love you,' she said softly, for perhaps only the second time, and he reached for her and pulled her close again.

Monday morning, and an early appointment at the mortuary. In all Webb's years as a police officer, this was his first post-mortem on a skeleton. He hoped it might be less stomach-churning than usual.

'We'd the devil of a job separating them,' one of the mortuary attendants had confided in the gowning-room. 'Took the best part of the weekend.'

Dr Stapleton, as at home with a skeleton as with the more usual cadaver, conducted the examination with his customary meticulousness, and Webb's hope of a stab wound was soon laid to rest. Without question, death had been caused by a severe blow to the skull, which had resulted in extensive fractures. For the rest, the dental records proved conclusively that it was Dick Vernon's remains which lay before them. Which was as well, since there was little else by which to identify him. All that had been found in the soil was a watch and a belt buckle, both badly corroded, a handful of coins and a few shirt buttons. The clothing itself had long since rotted, though possibly the lab might make something of the fibres.

And that was about it. With no organs to weigh or stomach contents to examine, the procedure was considerably shortened.

Webb approached the pathologist as he washed his hands at the sink. 'Could the injuries have been caused by falling heavily on a hard surface?' he inquired.

'Yes, it's possible. But since we have no brain matter we can't examine it for *contre-coup*, which is consistent with that type of impact.'

Which was not what Webb wanted to hear. 'How about a traffic accident?' he asked desperately, remembering Hannah's suggestion. 'Could he have been run over?'

Stapleton frowned. 'Extremely unlikely. There would have been multiple fractures throughout, and none of the other bones was damaged. What are you getting at, Chief Inspector?'

'Just scratching around.'

'Considering the state of the remains,' Stapleton said severely, 'we're fortunate to have any conclusive evidence.'

With which Webb could not argue. He left the mortuary and walked through the hospital grounds to the police station next door, where Jackson was waiting for him. Ten minutes later they were on their way back to Erlesborough.

'So he's been dead all this time.' Mrs Vernon was sitting straight-backed in her chair, her eyes dry and bright.

'I'm very sorry,' Webb said gently.

'Oh, I gave up hope years ago. At least he didn't leave me, as everyone thought; I'm glad of that.'

'Mrs Vernon, I know it's a long time ago, but I'll need a detailed account of the days leading up to your husband's disappearance. Who he spoke to, or about, where he went.'

With an effort she refocused on his face. 'That's no problem, they're ingrained in my memory; for months I went over and over those last few days, searching for a clue as to what happened. I didn't find one then, so I don't see how you can now.'

'How did he spend them?'

'With Joan, mostly.' Even now, there was a hint of resentment in her voice. 'When she was taken ill he went every day, though I kept begging him not to. There were the boys to consider, after all.'

To his embarrassment, Webb realized he did not know the cause of Joan Wainwright's death. 'The boys?' he repeated tentatively.

'Well, she was infectious, wasn't she?' And at his blank look, she said impatiently, 'German measles—we were in the midst of an epidemic. It's not usually serious unless you're pregnant, but she had complications, poor woman. She was never all that strong. I was sorry, afterwards, that

I'd not been more sympathetic. Still, that's water under the bridge now.'

'When did Mrs Wainwright become ill?'

'Only days before she died. That's why it was such a shock—it happened so quickly.'

'Could you be a little more exact, Mrs Vernon? According to her tombstone she died on the nineteenth of May. I've checked, and that was a Saturday. You're saying she was taken ill during that week?'

'Oh, definitely. We were all at a wedding the previous weekend and she seemed fine then, though of course she must have been incubating it.'

'Let's say, then, that she became ill on the Monday, which would have been the fourteenth, and your husband spent most of his time that week with her. What about after she died?'

'He was completely devastated.'

'But what did he do, Mrs Vernon?' Webb persisted. 'There were five days between her death and his disappearance. Where did he go and who did he see?'

She exclaimed impatiently, 'What can it possibly matter who—?' Then she broke off, and he saw the dawning horror in her eyes. She moistened suddenly dry lips and said in an entirely different voice, 'You must think me a fool. I've been so taken up with Dick's being found at last, I hadn't stopped to think what happened to him. But he was murdered, wasn't he? Like Billy Makepeace?'

'I'm afraid so, yes. So can you tell me, in as much detail as possible, what you remember of his last day?'

She was silent for a while, staring down at her clasped hands. Then she said slowly, 'It was the day after Joan's funeral. Dick was—beside himself. They'd always been close, and it's no use denying I resented that at times. When Joan died, it was as though a part of him had gone too.'

She drew a deep breath. 'The doctor'd given him sleeping pills, and he didn't wake till about ten that morning. There'd been a letter in the post from the bride's parents, enclosing a wedding photo. Joan was in the group, all happy and smiling. We'd not had time to let them know, you see. I managed to hide it before Dick came down, but unfortunately he found it later.' She stopped speaking, lost in the painful memories.

'And was his reaction as bad as you feared?' Webb prompted gently.

'Worse. He took it up to the bedroom and locked himself in.'

'What time of day was this?'

'After supper.'

'And when did he go out?'

'As soon as he came down. I was quite relieved; I thought the walk might do him good. He'd been mooching round all day, in and out of the garden, never staying anywhere long, unable to keep still. I tried to keep things as normal as possible, serving meals at the usual times and so on, but he didn't eat anything. Then he came downstairs with the photograph and told me he was going out for some cigarettes.'

'What time was this, Mrs Vernon?' Webb interrupted, mindful of Jackson's flying pen.

'Just after half past eight.'

'And where would he have gone for them?'

'Only to the Plough, at the end of the road. He quite often went there if he ran out, and stopped for a drink. I hoped he would that night—that it would take his mind off things for a while. But of course he never came home.'

'Had he called at the Plough?'

'No, no one had seen him. It's a complete mystery where he went.'

Not, Webb reflected wryly, to him. He knew to his cost that Vernon had gone to the old barn to meet his former sweetheart, and become embroiled in a fight with her husband. But what had happened next? That was the crucial point.

'And someone killed him,' Mrs Vernon ended flatly, as though answering his unspoken thought. 'It's—grotesque. Who would have wanted to do that?'

Her question hung in the air, seeming to Webb's guilty ears to hold a note of accusation as her eyes went past him to the framed photograph on the piano. As much to avoid answering her as from curiosity, he rose and went over to look at it. He saw a youngish, fair-haired man with regular features, smiling a little hesitantly, as though responding to a request from his unknown photographer. Impossible to think of him as a contemporary either of his father or of Billy Makepeace.

Staring at the photograph, Webb realized that in fact he thought of all three men as of different generations. His father was crystallized in his memory as he'd last seen him, a man in his late forties with already-thinning hair and grooves running from nose to bitter mouth. In the newspaper photograph Makepeace had been some thirty years older, heavy-jowled, grey-haired, with grizzled cheeks. Yet when this picture was taken, the other two had been equally young. Had one of them had a hand in Dick's death?

He turned, meeting Mrs Vernon's eyes and realizing that she was aware of at least some of what he'd been thinking.

'Who'd want to hurt Dick?' she challenged him, more directly this time.

'I don't know, Mrs Vernon,' Webb said quietly, 'but I intend to find out.'

For a moment longer she held his eyes and he braced himself for a specific accusation; but then she gave a little shrug and looked away. With a feeling of relief he signalled to Jackson and moved towards the door.

'We'll probably need to speak to you again, ma'am, but do contact us if you remember anything in the meantime.'

She accompanied them to the front door in silence and stood looking after them as they walked down the path. Webb hoped that the shock she'd received would jolt some hitherto dormant memory to the forefront of her mind.

Stanley Fox, treasurer of St Gabriel's church, let himself into his house and closed the door as thankfully as if he'd attained sanctuary. Yet even as the thought struck him, he acknowledged it was an illusion; the walls of this house weren't sacrosanct and there was nothing to stop either the vicar or the police from entering and asking questions.

Why, he thought agonizingly, had he ever touched the blasted money? He'd only *borrowed* it, for heaven's sake; in another month, when his policy matured, it would have been replaced, with no one any the wiser. At least, that had been the intention. But Makepeace was always an interfering old devil, with a nose for irregularities. Fox had no idea how he'd got on to him, and now he never would know, because Makepeace was dead. The fact struck him each time with a fresh sense of shock.

'Stanley—' His wife was coming downstairs, carrying their youngest grandchild. 'Have you heard the news?'

'How do I know until you tell me?' he answered testily, making for the whisky bottle in the dining-room sideboard. She followed him, still holding the child, and watched from the doorway as he poured himself a tot. Aware of her presence, he turned, lifting the bottle inquiringly, and she shook her head. 'Not at this time of day, and nor should you. I don't know what's got into you this last week.'

He tossed back the whisky and wiped his mouth with the back of his hand. 'So what's your news then?'

'They've found Dick Vernon.'

'*Dick Vernon?*' He gazed at her incredulously, momentarily diverted from his own worries. 'Good grief! Don't tell me he's turned up after all these years?'

Mrs Fox set the child down and gave it a gentle little push in the direction of the sitting-room. 'In a manner of speaking,' she said quietly. 'At least, his body has—in his sister's grave. He'd been murdered, Stanley. Isn't it terrible, him as well as Mr Makepeace?'

Fox fumbled again for the whisky bottle. 'But the police were called in over Makepeace's death; what made them start digging in the cemetery?'

'I don't know, I'm sure.' She shuddered. 'This has always been such a pleasant place to live, and now, all at once, two murders. I've told Marion to collect the children from school until they catch him. You never know what might happen.'

'There may be two murders, Mary, but they're forty years apart, remember. It can hardly be considered a crime-wave.'

'I suppose you're right,' she said doubtfully. 'All the same, it won't do any harm to be extra careful for a while. Now, put that bottle away and go and keep an eye on Daniel while I get the lunch.'

Webb said, 'Yes, Dr Adams, that's quite correct . . . No, there's no doubt about his identity; fortunately we had his dental records, or we might have had a problem . . . Fractured skull. The ubiquitous blunt instrument, no doubt. Little chance of finding *that* after forty years!'

Webb looked up at Jackson with a little grimace as the doctor's voice continued over the wire. 'I see. I'm sorry, I didn't realize she was your patient . . . Yes, of course . . . Actually, she took it very well; she must have accepted he was dead years ago . . . Yes, I'm sure a visit would be appreciated.'

'A short lesson in medical ethics,' Webb said ruefully as he put down the phone. 'The good doctor feels we should have contacted him before going to Mrs Vernon, so he could have been standing by. Mind you, she's a pretty tough cookie, that one. Now, Ken, just two quick phone calls, then we'll break for lunch.'

At The Old Farmhouse the phone rang just as the meal had been served, and Sheila went to answer it. She was gone for several minutes, and returned looking pale.

'Who was it?' Colin asked.

'David, confirming that they'd found Dick Vernon. He promised to let me know.'

'So that's that. End of one mystery, start of another— who killed *him?*' He looked up at her as she stood staring out of the window. 'Well, sit down then, and get on with your meal.'

Absent-mindedly she resumed her place, though she didn't pick up her fork.

'What is it, Sheila?'

'Nothing really, I suppose. Just that the other evening David warned me not to mention what I'd seen in the cemetery, nor that Mr Makepeace had phoned.'

'Why?' Stephen was intrigued by his mother's part in the investigation.

'That's just it; I didn't ask then, so I did now. And he said that whoever killed Mr Makepeace might have done so because he repeated what I'd said.'

There was a short silence. Then Colin said hesitantly, 'Does that mean you're in danger?'

'He didn't actually say so, but how can I be? It's not as if I could identify anyone. I thought I'd seen a *ghost!*' Suddenly she put her head in her hands. 'God, why did I ever mention it? If I hadn't, Mr Makepeace might still be alive and Dick Vernon safely buried, where he was no danger to anyone.'

Colin patted her arm automatically, but his eyes were troubled. It occurred to him that if Makepeace had indeed died because of what Sheila'd said, he would undoubtedly have passed on the source of his information.

CHAPTER 10

'It'll mean retracing our steps, Ken,' Webb said resignedly over lunch at the Narrow Boat. 'We now need to check what people were doing when Dick Vernon disappeared, as well as the night Billy died. I've been through the original files, but I'd say it's quite likely a number of those interviewed are no longer with us.'

Including his parents, Webb reflected. He had noted grimly that neither John nor Lilian Webb had admitted seeing Dick Vernon the night he vanished.

'For the rest,' he continued, 'it'll be interesting to compare the earlier statements with what they say now. We can also interview the younger ones, who were kids at the time. They might remember something if we ask the right questions.'

'You still think the deaths are connected, Guv?' Jackson inquired, spearing a sausage.

'It's the hell of a coincidence if they're not. Mind, that's not to say the same person killed them both.'

'Meaning Makepeace could still have murdered Vernon?'

Webb said evenly, 'Or my father could.'

Jackson shot him a startled glance, decided he was joking, and smiled uncertainly.

'As regards Makepeace,' Webb continued, 'suppose he actually did kill Dick, and the Vernon boys have just got wind of it?'

'And avenged their father's death after forty years?' Jackson's doubts were evident in his voice.

'There'd have to be more to it than that,' Webb agreed, 'but it could be a starting point.'

'So who do we see first?'

'Sam Wainwright. One of my calls just now was to the vicar; we've fixed the reinterment for nine in the morning.'

It took several minutes for their knock to be answered, and Mrs Wainwright apologized for keeping them waiting.

'We're in the back garden,' she explained, leading them through the house and out of the open french windows. Her husband, resplendent in Panama hat, was in a deckchair in the shade of a cherry tree. He looked up from his paper, watching suspiciously as they approached across the grass.

Mrs Wainwright had paused on the terrace to collect two collapsible chairs, which she now set up alongside the others. Unfortunately they were outside the patch of shade.

'You'll no doubt have heard about your brother-in-law,' Webb began as he seated himself.

'Yes,' the old man said gruffly. 'I reckon I owe you an apology; you knew what you were doing after all. I'm damned if I know what put you on to it, though?' His voice ended interrogatively, but Webb offered no explanation.

'My main reason for calling is to tell you that your first wife will be reburied tomorrow morning. We thought it best to make it early, so the service can be as private as possible.'

'Service?'

'The vicar will be present, to say a few words.'

'That's nice,' the second Mrs Wainwright said softly, and after a moment her husband nodded agreement.

'I hope nine o'clock's convenient. We can send a car for you, if you'd like?'

'That's all right, Chief Inspector.' Again it was the woman who spoke. 'I'll drive us down, thanks all the same.' She paused. 'You said that was your main reason for coming; have you something else to tell us?'

'It's more a question of asking, Mrs Wainwright. I'm afraid we need to know what your husband remembers of the days leading up to Mr Vernon's disappearance. I'm sorry if it brings back painful memories.'

'I went through it all at the time,' Sam said wearily.

'I know, sir, but it's a murder inquiry now.'

'Well, as I said before, there's little to tell. From the time Joan was taken ill, Dick spent most of his time with her, in the bedroom up there.'

'She died of German measles, I believe?' Webb prompted gently.

'Yes, though there was some fancy name on the death certificate.'

'Encephalitis,' his wife supplied. 'Inflammation of the brain. You sometimes get it with measles or German measles. There's no treatment for it.'

'And it came on very suddenly?'

Wainwright nodded, staring down at the grass. 'We'd been to a wedding the previous Saturday and she was right as rain.'

Jackson looked up from his notebook. 'Excuse me, sir— He glanced at Webb, who nodded to him to continue. 'Mrs Vernon was saying the bride's parents didn't know of her death—they sent a photo which arrived after the funeral.'

Wainwright frowned. 'Well?'

'Well, sir, I was wondering where the wedding took place? I mean, if it had been local, surely they'd have heard?'

'But it wasn't local, Sergeant, it was in Swansea. On Whit Saturday—when we still had Christian holidays in May, not ruddy Communist ones. We all went over for the weekend—Dick and Eileen and Joan and me. Stayed till the Monday, in fact, and it was when we got back that Joan complained of a headache. We thought it was all the travelling.'

'And Mr Vernon visited her regularly while she was ill?'

'Visited? He practically moved in! Apart from going home to sleep, he was here all the time—and I think if I'd let him, he'd have spent the nights here too.'

'Since he and his sister were so close, I suppose you'd always seen quite a lot of him?'

'A fair bit, but every now and then Eileen put her foot down, and I must say I agreed with her.'

'So you'd have known if he had any enemies?'

Wainwright looked up, his old eyes shrewd. 'You're asking me that, Davy Webb? He was engaged to your mother once. I bet you never knew that.'

Webb was aware of Jackson's surprise. 'Not until last week. But apart from my father and Billy Makepeace, was there anyone else he didn't get on with?'

Wainwright shook his head decidedly. 'He was the most easygoing of chaps, Dick. Everybody liked him.' He looked challengingly at Webb but, remembering the diffidently smiling photograph, he made no attempt to dispute it.

'Did you see him between your wife's death and her funeral?'

'No, nor did I expect to.'

Mrs Wainwright, who had slipped away during the previous exchange, now reappeared with a tray bearing four glasses and a jug of homemade lemonade. 'Can I offer you a cold drink, Chief Inspector?'

Webb accepted gratefully. His jacket and tie were not ideal wear for sitting in the garden and, in the full glare of the sun, he was uncomfortably hot. As he sipped the drink, the ice clinking against the glass, he looked about him at the neat lawn, the colourful beds, shrubs and rockery. Sam Wainwright had lived here with his first wife. Perhaps it was she who had planted some of the trees which now bent gracefully over the garden. Poor Joan Wainwright who, with her twin brother, had died at the early age of thirty-eight.

He drained his glass and stood up. 'Thank you both for your help, specially since this is such a difficult time for you.'

'And for you, lad,' Wainwright acknowledged gruffly. 'I'll be glad when it's all over, as I'm sure you will.'

Indeed he would, Webb thought feelingly, unless he finished by proving his own father's guilt.

By way of tackling the most difficult interviews first, Webb next phoned the Vernon brothers, but both were out of town at a meeting. He wondered if they'd heard their father'd been identified.

By default, therefore, priority passed to a return call on Mrs Makepeace. Webb hoped Jenny'd not be there; he'd been clumsy in his questioning of her, and he knew his abrupt departure while she was still upset had been due more to cold feet than professionalism.

When they drew up at Longacre Farm, Dr Adams's blue Cavalier was parked in the yard. Webb hesitated, wondering if it was a routine visit or if the old woman had been taken ill. But as he and Jackson got out of the car, the door of the house opened and Jenny showed the doctor out. Even across the yard, Webb saw her stiffen as she caught sight of him. He waited by the gate as the doctor came towards them looking cool and dapper in his light suit, a flower as always in his buttonhole. By contrast Webb felt even more crumpled—but then the doctor hadn't spent half an hour in a sun-baked garden probing painful memories.

'Good afternoon, Chief Inspector. How are your inquiries going?'

'Slowly, doctor, as is usually the way.' He paused. 'Did you check on Mrs Vernon?'

'Yes, she's bearing up well. As you say, she probably resigned herself years ago. It's a gruesome thought, though, the poor chap lying there just below the surface all these years.'

'Did you know him and his sister?'

'Only vaguely; they were Dr Nairn's patients, and it all happened soon after I came here. I remember the hoo-ha when he disappeared, though.'

From the corner of his eye Webb noticed that Jenny, after waiting for a moment, had retreated inside and the door was firmly closed again. He nodded in its direction.

'Mrs Makepeace all right?'

'Well, she's very frail. Even before all this, she was fading pretty rapidly.'

'Would a few more questions hurt her?'

'I shouldn't think so, but keep them as short as you can. She tires very easily.'

Webb nodded, and as the doctor got into his car, he and Jackson approached the farmhouse. Jenny let them wait several minutes before she answered their ring.

'I'm sorry to trouble you again, Mrs Hawthorn, but as you've no doubt heard, another case has come up and we've a few more questions for your mother. And you too, perhaps.'

She lifted an eyebrow. 'Very well.'

Mrs Makepeace was in exactly the same position as they'd last seen her. Jackson wondered if she'd been out of her chair at all in the interim. As before, Webb drew a chair up to her side.

'Hello, Mrs Makepeace, it's David Webb again.'

She peered at him with her milky eyes. 'Have you found out who killed Billy?'

'Not yet, I'm afraid.'

'Jenny told you about those phone-calls?'

'Yes, thank you. We're working on them.' He paused. 'I suppose you've heard about Dick Vernon?'

She sighed. 'Yes, that's a bad business.'

'Do you remember anything about the time he dis-appeared?'

'Only coppers coming round asking if we'd seen him.'

'But I don't suppose you had?'

'No. We didn't even go to Joan's funeral. We wouldn't have been welcome.'

Webb framed his words carefully, aware of Jenny's hos-tile attention. 'Did your husband have any theories on what might have happened?'

'We talked about it, of course. Some folks thought he'd lost his memory, what with the shock of it all, and wandered off, not knowing who he was.'

'Did your husband go along with that?'

Mrs Makepeace shrugged. 'He'd nothing better to suggest.'

'He never mentioned any talk he'd overheard which might have thrown a different light on it? Gossip at the Farmers' Club or the church?'

'Not that I recall.'

Webb swivelled in his chair to look up at Jenny, who, he guessed, had deliberately remained standing in order to make him uncomfortable.

'How much do you remember, Mrs Hawthorn?'

'The same as you, I should think. Being told at school to be nice to the Vernon boys and not to mention their father. But we never spoke to them anyway, did we? We weren't allowed to, any more than we could talk to each other.'

The old woman shook her head sadly and Jenny added reflectively, 'We played games all that term, about people disappearing and the things that might happen to them.'

Her words brought back that long-ago summer and the similar games he and his friends had played. But of all the wild possibilities they'd dreamed up—including kidnap by spacemen or Russian spies—they'd not thought of burial in someone else's grave.

Mrs Makepeace said suddenly, 'When can we have Billy back? It's only right he should be decently buried.'

'Just as soon as the Coroner releases him, Mrs Make-peace.' Which, Webb thought darkly, depended on how the investigation went.

He'd not expected to learn anything about Dick Vernon in this household; if Makepeace had killed him, he wouldn't have come home and told his family. Still, it had had to be checked. Stifling a sigh, he stood up, replaced the upright chair against the wall and, nodding to Jackson, took his leave.

Sheila stood behind the counter in the gift shop, watching the crowds moving about outside the window. It had been a fairly busy afternoon, but now only one woman was left in here, hesitating by the flower-arranging stand. Sheila wished she'd make up her mind and go. It was nearly closing time, for which she was profoundly grateful. All afternoon she'd been on edge, furtively watching people to see if they were watching her. Suppose Mr Makepeace's killer was mingling with those aimless crowds? Or was he —or she—someone she knew?

The customer approached at last and, smiling fixedly, Sheila took from her the heavy oblong pinholder and the block of oasis, clocked up the prices and handed over the change. Dropping the purchases into a bag, she passed it across and, as the woman left, followed her to the door. Across the way, Stephen was locking up the garden furni-ture showroom. He waved to her through the glass and she raised a hand in reply as she started to close the door.

'Sheila!'

She jumped, heart accelerating, and turned to see David walking quickly towards her. He smiled. 'I thought I was going to be locked out! Colin told me you were here.'

'Come in quickly, then, I don't want any more cus-tomers.'

He followed her into the building and she locked the door behind him. She felt safer with David, able to relax for the first time since lunch. 'What can I do for you?'

'Put me up again tonight, if you would. Mrs Wainwright's being reinterred at nine in the morning. At least I won't have to creep out at four this time!'

'No problem. Your bed's still made up.'

'I've also a few more questions, I'm afraid. Are you coming back to the house?'

'Not until I've checked the till. But we can talk here if you like. At least it's private.'

'OK.' He perched on the counter. 'I'm sorry to keep harping on the day Dick disappeared but, as you'll appreciate, it's even more important now.'

'I've told you all I can remember.'

'There are one or two points I'm not clear on. You say you had a picnic tea that day. Who was there?'

'Just a few kids from the playgroup—and Mum, of course.'

'No other adults?'

'No.'

'What time did you get home?'

'About six, I suppose. Not long before my bedtime.'

'Was Father in?'

'He was working in the garden. I ran out to tell him about the picnic.'

Webb was silent, envying his sister her happy relationship with their father which had been denied to himself. Briefly he was tempted to tell her what he'd seen in the barn that night, but he resisted. No point in worrying her at this stage. He said merely, 'He went out later, though, didn't he?'

'Did he? I don't remember. He might have gone bowling.'

'I remember when I crept out myself, Mother was in the kitchen with the girl next door. What was her name?'

'Mavis. Yes, I remember now. She brought my present round and we gave her some birthday cake.'

'Had she come to babysit, do you think? If Mother was going to meet Dick, she wouldn't have left us alone.'

Sheila said slowly, 'I never thought of that. I wonder if she'll remember, after all this time.'

Webb looked at her in surprise. 'You're still in touch with her?'

'Oh yes. Well, I don't see much of her, but she used to babysit for us when the children were younger. She was always mad on babies, it was too bad she never had any of her own. She married a widower twenty years older, but it seemed to work out.'

Webb fished in his pocket for his notebook. 'Could you give me her married name and phone number?'

Sheila did so. 'You think she might help?'

'Goodness knows, but it's worth a try.'

She nodded. 'Well, if that's all, I'd better add up our takings. Go back to the house, David, and Colin'll give you a drink. I shan't be long.'

Colin, pouring the drinks with his back to Webb, said evenly, 'Yes, as it happens I do remember that day. I was quite friendly with the Vernons then, before I inherited Sheila's taboo. Their mother rang mine and asked if they could come to tea after school. Apparently Dick was distraught and she thought it best to keep the boys out of his way.'

Webb stared at his back. 'Why the hell didn't you say so before?'

'Because it hasn't the slightest bearing on anything.'

'That's for me to decide,' Webb said stiffly.

'Well, I'm sorry.' Colin turned and came over with the glasses, not meeting his eyes. 'Quite honestly, I've always resented this feud nonsense. It was nothing to do with me, but I feel embarrassed even mentioning the Vernons or the Makepeaces to you and Sheila.'

Webb studied him as he seated himself in his armchair and crossed his legs. Colin Fairchild, the solicitor's son, whom he had known most of his life. But not very well, he now realized. Colin's tanned face was slightly flushed and his mouth set. Webb had always thought him pleasant and easygoing, but this was the man who had defied his father and given up university to open a garden centre. He was a a more determined character than his brother-in-law had given him credit for. In the still youthful-looking man, Webb could see the curly-haired boy who had played cricket for Greystones' first eleven, been school captain, achieved high examination results. Did he ever regret missed opportunities, wish he had after all followed his father into the law firm?

Webb sipped his drink. 'And did the boys say anything the next day?'

Colin looked up, seeming grateful that the status quo had been restored. 'Only that their father had gone away for a few days, which was what their mother had told them.'

'Did they ever mention his going out that evening?'

'Not in my hearing. In fact, I never heard them speak of him again. I think they thought he'd deserted them.' Colin swirled his drink reflectively. 'I remember Dick Vernon, too. He used to play cricket with us in the garden. I liked him.'

'Did you also like Billy Makepeace?' Webb asked evenly.

Colin said quickly, 'Look, I'm not—'

Webb lifted a hand. 'Seriously, I want to know. Did you?'

'He was all right.'

'You didn't speak to him when he phoned Sheila?'

'No, I was—' Colin broke off, and the flush which had faded from his face returned. 'Lyn took the call,' he ended lamely.

'You were out?'

'Yes. Yes, I was, as a matter of fact.'

'Where?'

The flush deepened, but Webb waited impassively. Incredible that somehow, despite the intensive questioning, he'd not established where Colin had been that evening.

'There was an Old Boys' Dinner at Greystones.'

'A late do, I suppose?'

'Yes; Sheila was in bed when I got back.'

Webb looked at him curiously. For some reason, Colin was acutely uncomfortable. He wondered why.

'You've kept in touch with the school, then. I must confess I've never gone to any of the Grammar School shindigs.'

Colin made no comment, keeping his eyes on his drink. It would do no harm, Webb reflected, to check that his brother-in-law had attended the Dinner. God, if this case wasn't wrapped up quickly he'd have alienated his entire family.

He finished his drink and stood up. 'I think if you'll excuse me I'll go and have a quick sluice. I've spent far too much time in the sun today and my clothes are sticking to me.'

Colin nodded, looking broodingly after him as he left the room. That was a bloody stupid thing to say, he realized. David was nothing if not thorough, and a quick call to the school would soon reveal he hadn't been at the Dinner. Not, to be pedantic, that he'd actually said he had.

He got up abruptly and went to refill his glass. It was the question about taking the phone-call that had thrown him; on David's first visit, he'd been ready with a plausible story if asked to account for his movements. To his surprised relief he had not been, and he'd foolishly thought the danger past.

What damnable timing it had been! he thought with a rush of fury, splashing soda into his glass. That night of all nights! He thought of Billy Makepeace, who had had no right to be where he was, of his initial surprise and then the slow, knowing smile that spread over his face.

Hardly knowing what he was doing, Colin tossed the whisky back in one gulp and stood with his head flung back, gazing up at the ceiling. Then, hearing his wife's voice in the hall, he slowly straightened and went to meet her.

There was quite a group at the graveside the next morning when Webb arrived with DC Charlton. In addition to Sam Wainwright and his wife, the family was represented by Mrs Vernon and her two sons and daughters-in-law.

Webb studied the younger women with interest; the one standing by Larry he did not know, but the other seemed familiar. He'd seen her somewhere, he was sure of it. There was no mistaking those green eyes and the heavy red-gold hair. Then, all at once, he remembered. Rona Seton, she'd been, and her arrival in town at the age of sixteen had caused a stir among the lads. So she'd married Tom Vernon. Well, well.

Becoming aware of his glance, the woman looked across, meeting his eye and then quickly dropping her own as a faint flush touched her face. Webb was intrigued. A poised and confident woman in her forties, she must be used to men's attention. So what, he wondered, had caused her embarrassment? Surely nothing as banal as the family feud?

The brief graveside service began. The family throughout was solemn but composed—this was no new grief. Surprisingly, the only tears Webb saw were in the eyes of the second Mrs Wainwright as the shining new coffin was lowered into the cavity in which its occupant had, with her twin brother, spent the last forty years. She would not be disturbed again.

Old Sam bent stiffly to pick up a handful of earth and throw it into the grave, where it rattled on the wooden lid, an accompaniment to the vicar's rhythmic words. Then, with his wife holding tightly to his arm, he turned away, glancing briefly at the two wreaths which lay on the grass.

Webb intercepted the Vernon brothers as they started to follow him. 'You'll appreciate, gentlemen, that I'll need to see you again in the light of your father's death. Would this evening be convenient? At home, perhaps?' He'd like a word with the wives, too, he thought, registering the startled jerk of Rona's head, as if she divined his purpose.

'If you must, you must,' her husband said ungraciously. 'You and Frances come too, Larry, so we can get it all over at once.'

'Six o'clock?' Webb suggested. After which, he could go home. He didn't want another evening with his family.

'Very well, we'll be waiting. Now, if you'll excuse us—'

And, taking his wife's arm, Vernon followed the rest of the mourners out of the cemetery.

CHAPTER 11

After leaving the cemetery, Webb returned with DI Charlton to Silver Street, where he'd arranged to pick up Jackson.

'There are a couple of things I want to do on the Makepeace case, Ken. Then I propose to shelve it for the rest of the day and concentrate on Dick Vernon. It could well be, anyway, that approaching from a different angle will lead us to Makepeace's killer. So first we'll go to see the solicitor who found him, then I'd like you to phone Greystones College and check whether Mr Colin Fairchild attended their Old Boys' Dinner on Monday last week.'

Jackson shot him a startled glance. That would be the Governor's brother-in-law, surely? No wonder he hadn't wanted to get involved in this case. Feeling a verbal reply might be imprudent, he merely nodded and adjusted his step to his superior's long stride as they set off for the High Street.

Martin Allerdyce, junior partner in the law firm of Henshaw & Allerdyce, was a pleasant-faced man in his late thirties with thinning fair hair and horn-rimmed spectacles. He nodded to Jackson, whom he'd met before, and shook Webb's hand.

'I'm afraid, Chief Inspector, I've really nothing to add to what I told your sergeant here the other day. It fell to me to find the poor chap, and I just did the necessary, that's all.'

'All the same, I'd be glad of a more detailed account, sir. For instance, how did you come to see him? Did you recognize him at once? Try to pull him out of the water?'

'Oh, I see. Well, I was walking along the towpath on my way to work and as I reached the railway bridge I heard a train coming. It makes one hell of a din if you're underneath the bridge when it goes over, so I paused to wait for it to pass, and happened to glance down at the canal. I saw him at once and it was a shock, I can tell you—the calm, shining water, the flowers on the bank, and then, suddenly, this floating bundle of clothes. Because of course I knew it was more than clothes.

'I bent down and pulled the body closer in to the bank, and to answer your question, no, at that stage I didn't recognize him—he was floating face down. I struggled to turn him over, chiefly to get his face out of the water, but it wasn't easy because his clothes were waterlogged. I did manage to turn him far enough (a) to recognize him and (b) to see he was dead. I went on struggling for a while in case there was a chance of artificial respiration, but he was too heavy for me. I had my mobile phone, so I rang the police and Dr Adams.'

'And waited till they arrived at the scene?'

'Yes. I made a statement to PC Stebbins, but I'd a nine-thirty appointment so I left straight afterwards.'

'I understand Mr Makepeace was your client, sir.'

'That's right.'

'Had you been acting for him long?'

'The firm has, for many years. I took over when Mr Henshaw senior retired.'

'Mr Makepeace didn't by any chance leave any sealed packets or envelopes with you, to be opened after his death?'

The solicitor shook his head. 'No, nothing.'

'But you hold a copy of his will, no doubt.'

The man hesitated. 'Yes.'

'Can you tell me offhand when it was dated?'

'Thirtieth October, nineteen eighty-six.'

'And have there been any additions or changes since then?'

The solicitor cleared his throat. 'There was one recent codicil, yes.'

'Concerning his daughter?'

'No.'

'Mr Allerdyce,' Webb said gently, 'this is a murder case, you know.'

'I'm sorry. It—goes against the grain to discuss clients' affairs. The codicil concerned Mr Jeremy Croft.'

'Ah!'

'As it happens,' the solicitor went on hurriedly, 'I'm expecting Mrs Hawthorn any minute for a reading of the will. I did offer to go to Longacre so her mother could be present, but the old lady knows the general terms and isn't interested in details.'

The codicil could be of supreme importance; primed of it, Webb fully intended to sit in on the reading, but he'd wait till Jenny arrived before broaching the subject.

He changed his angle, feeling the man's relief. 'When did you last see Mr Makepeace, sir? Alive, that is?'

'A month ago. He came in about some property he wanted to sell.' The intercom on the desk buzzed and Allerdyce lifted the phone and listened to a voice over the wire. 'Right, thank you. I'll be out in a moment.' He looked at Webb. 'Mrs Hawthorn has arrived, Chief Inspector, so if there's nothing else?'

Webb stood and Jackson with him, and allowed the solicitor to show them to the door. Jenny, standing by the desk in the foyer, widened her eyes at the sight of him. Before Allerdyce could speak, Webb said smoothly, 'Mrs Hawthorn, I believe you're here for the reading of your father's will? I'm sure that in the circumstances you'd have no objection to my being present?'

Allerdyce gasped and started to protest, but Jenny said coldly, 'It's all right, Mr Allerdyce. I have no objection.'

Webb turned to Jackson. 'Sergeant, would you go and make the phone call we were discussing earlier? I'll see you back at the station.'

Allerdyce was saying stiffly, 'I'm sorry, Mrs Hawthorn. Mr Webb gave me no inkling he was going to make that request.'

She shrugged. 'I'm not expecting any dramatic revelations. If the Chief Inspector wants to listen, it makes no difference to me.'

She walked past Webb without looking at him and seated

herself in the chair he'd just vacated. Webb sat down in Jackson's place.

The main part of the will, read slowly in the usual contorted language, was as expected. The bulk of the estate, including the farm and buildings, was left to his wife during her lifetime and after her death to his daughter. Various bequests were made to friends, a couple of charities, and a substantial sum to St Gabriel's church.

'We now come to the codicil, dated six months ago,' Allerdyce said, with a cool glance in Webb's direction. '"I hereby write off the loan of £25,000 made to my employee Mr Jeremy Croft of Longacre Bungalow, Oxbury Road, Erlesborough, together with all interest accruing, and direct that any repayments made by him on said loan at the time of my death shall be repaid to him in full."'

Allerdyce looked up, surveying the two surprised faces. 'An extremely generous settlement, I'm sure you will agree,' he said quietly.

That was an understatement. Despite his grouchiness and fault-finding, the old man had effectively paid in full the nursing-home fees required by Croft's mother, while the reimbursement of repayments already made would be a further considerable bonus. Which, Webb reflected, bore out what Lang had said about his old friend. Billy might be short-tempered and outspoken, but he was always ready to help those in genuine trouble. His private reflection was echoed by Jenny.

'That's typical of my father,' she said unsteadily. Then she turned to Webb, her eyes bright with unshed tears. 'Are you satisfied, Chief Inspector? Because if so, I'd be grateful of a few words in private with my solicitor.'

'Of course. Thank you for your cooperation, Mrs Hawthorn, Mr Allerdyce.' And Webb, rather thankfully, took his leave.

As he crossed the road on the way to Silver Street, he imagined the overwhelming easing of tension in the Croft household once the terms of the will were made known.

Provided, of course, Croft had not been the one who tipped his employer into the canal.

Jackson greeted Webb with the not altogether surprising news that Colin had not been at the Old Boys' Dinner. 'It took several phone-calls,' he informed him. 'The school itself didn't know, and I had to get on to the secretary of the Old Boys' Association, who was difficult to track down. Still, I got him eventually, and he was quite definite. Mr Fairchild had originally applied for a ticket, but rang up the week before to cancel it.' Jackson wondered anxiously if this was the news the Governor wanted. His expression gave nothing away.

'Right,' Webb said evenly, 'we'll now turn to Dick Vernon. We've spoken to the family about the day he disappeared. Now we must start on friends, acquaintances, business colleagues and so on. Mr Harvey's original list will be a starting point. First, though, I must arrange to see a lady who might be able to help—a Mrs Parker.' Mavis, the erstwhile 'girl next door', who had come to the Webb house on that fatal night.

He dialled the number Sheila had supplied, giving his official title and hoping she would not make the connection. It seemed she didn't. Sounding apprehensive but also quite excited, she agreed to see the detectives at three o'clock that afternoon.

The rest of the morning was spent in the tedious but necessary task of calling on people who had figured in the original investigation. There was one advantage; it appeared that in the same way as people the world over remembered what they were doing when President Kennedy was assassinated, so the inhabitants of Erlesborough recalled the day Dick Vernon vanished. Partly, no doubt, this was due to the interviews which had followed immediately afterward, but each had emblazoned on his or her memory the last time they'd seen the doomed man or the last words they'd exchanged.

Although it was now a murder case and Webb asked

slightly different questions from his predecessor, most wit-
nesses stuck pretty close to their original statements and
only a few unimportant facts emerged. It was also necessary
to make allowances for the tricks a self-dramatizing memory
could play on the most genuine people. Webb could only
hope those recollections, taken *en masse*, would prove a more
valuable source of information than they had forty years
ago.

The main obstacle was the seemingly total lack of motive,
and he wondered despairingly if his father had been the
only person to have one.

Yet as he continued diligently with these interviews,
Webb's thoughts turned more than once to Jenny Hawthorn, her rigid control during the reading of the will and
her trembling voice at the end of it. He regretted the hostility which had developed between them, and wondered if
there were some way he could dispel it. If she could be
persuaded to have lunch with him, perhaps they could talk
things through and reach a more amicable basis. After all,
they were both anxious to find her father's killer.

'Could you make your own arrangements for lunch,
Ken?' he said therefore, just before one o'clock. 'There's
someone I need to see. I'll be at the station by two-thirty,
in good time for our appointment with Mrs Parker.'

Another of the Governor's walkabouts, Jackson thought
resignedly.

The Sandon Arms was a smaller hotel than the Crown
at the other end of the High Street, but Webb remembered
it had had a good name in his youth. He thought briefly of
the family it was named after, whom he had interviewed
during the course of the nursery-rhyme case; then, as he
entered the foyer, forgot them as he looked round for Jenny.

There was no sign of her. Another receptionist, bright
and efficient, sat at the desk. 'Yes, sir? Can I help you?'

'I'm looking for Mrs Hawthorn,' he said.

Her face sobered. 'Are you a personal friend, sir?'

'Yes,' said Webb, without compunction.

'Well, she's gone home. She went to hear her father's will

read, and was rather upset when she got back so the manager gave her the rest of the day off.'

Webb cursed silently. 'She'll have gone back to the farm, then?'

The girl hesitated. 'Since you're a friend, I don't suppose she'd mind me telling you. She's at her flat. I think she needed to be alone.'

'Her flat?' Would his pose as a friend be blown?

'That's right,' the receptionist said, innocently helping him out. 'Number forty-three, just round the corner.'

'Of course. Thanks, I'm most grateful.'

There was only one road 'just round the corner' from the Sandon, and that was Canal Street, which separated the hotel from La Brioche café. It ran parallel to Silver Street further up the High Street, but whereas the latter ended in a stone wall overlooking the canal, this road petered out into a footpath leading down to the water. Webb turned into it, located No. 43, checked the names on the bell-push and rang the appropriate bell. After a moment a clogged voice said, 'Who is it?'

'David Webb.'

There was a long silence. Then: 'What do you want?' She sounded as if she'd been crying.

'To see you, Jenny. Please.'

Another pause, then a buzz sounded and the front door opened to his push. Her flat was on the first floor of the converted house. He entered the hallway and walked up the broad staircase. The door at the top of the stairs opened as he reached it and Jenny stood there looking at him in silence, her eyes red and swollen, her hair tousled. He gently took her arm and led her back inside.

She said flatly, 'I'm sorry it's stuffy. I've opened all the windows, but I haven't been here for a week.'

'Have you had lunch?' He doubted if she'd agree to go out for it, looking as she did.

'I'm not hungry.

'Any food in the flat?'

'No, I emptied the fridge when I went to Mum's.'

'Then wait here and I'll bring something back. You need to eat.'

She made no reply and he ran back down the stairs and up to the High Street, grateful now for the proliferation of eating places. Minutes later he was back with a selection of freshly made sandwiches and a bottle of wine, and she watched in silence as he set the food out on the table by the window.

'Why are you doing this?' she asked dully.

'Because there seems to be no one else to look after you.'

She bit her lip, and said defensively, 'I thought I was one of your suspects?'

'No more than the rest of Erlesborough.'

She smiled unwillingly.

'That's better. Now come and sit down and let's see what this wine's like.'

Gradually, as she found she could after all eat, she began to relax and the mottled red faded from face and eyes. Webb kept up an inconsequential commentary, talking lightly of Dick Vernon rather than her father, since he'd no wish to precipitate more tears.

'The Vernon wives were at the service this morning,' he said. 'I didn't realize Tom had married the delectable Rona Seton.'

She nodded. 'Do you remember when she and her family arrived here? She was much more sophisticated than the rest of us, wearing make-up and so on.'

'I remember.'

'I was afraid you might fall for her!' she said.

He looked at her quickly, not sure where such reminiscences might lead. 'All the boys did, briefly, though I don't remember her looking in Tom Vernon's direction. Mind you, he was small and spotty at the time.'

She smiled. 'Have you spoken to her?'

'No, I'm going round there this evening.'

'She won't be much help. Dick had long gone by the time she got here.'

'But she was around when your father was killed.'

Jenny looked at him frowningly. 'Which case are you working on, then?'

'Both. I'm almost sure they're connected.'

That startled her. 'But how can they be?' Then she stiffened. 'You don't think Dad—?'

He laid a quick hand over hers. 'Steady now; don't start getting all prickly again. Jenny, haven't you wondered why your father phoned Sheila the night he died?'

'Of course I have, endlessly.' Her eyes widened. 'Do you know?'

'I think so.' Briefly, he told her the story of the conversation in the café before her arrival, which no doubt accounted for her father's absent-mindedness: and, when she still didn't understand, the interpretation he'd put on Sheila's ghost.

'And Dad reached the same conclusion?'

'I think so. Unfortunately he went and told the wrong person.'

After a moment she said, 'Thank you for telling me. I hope you're right; I'd rather he died for something he knew than because someone hated him. Illogical, but there it is. And thanks, too, for this.' Her gesture took in the remains of the meal. 'I do appreciate it. It's not easy, sometimes, being alone.'

He could think of nothing to say and she added, 'Didn't I hear your marriage broke up?'

'That's right, some years ago.'

'So did mine.'

'I'm sorry.'

'Is there anyone else on the scene?'

Webb thought gratefully of Hannah. 'Yes, though we've no plans to marry.'

'You're happy, though?'

'I suppose so, yes.' He did not dare return the question. The atmosphere during the last few moments had changed, and was becoming dangerous. He glanced surreptitiously at his watch and, catching him doing so, she smiled wryly and pushed back her chair.

'I mustn't keep you any longer, I've interrupted your day quite enough. I'm glad, though, that we're friends again.'

'Me too,' he said inanely. They moved towards the door, but as she reached to open it, he caught her hand on impulse and she turned inquiringly. Gently, unhurriedly, he took her in his arms and kissed her. It was the farewell they'd been denied all those years ago, a gentle letting-go of an adolescent dream, with no demands left on either side.

She was smiling as he released her, and he saw to his relief that she felt as he did. 'Bless you, Jenny,' he said softly.

'You too.'

'Take care.'

'Yes. And good luck with the case.'

He nodded and, without looking back, ran down the stairs and out on to the sunny street.

Mavis Parker, now a widow, lived up Glebe Hill, not far from the sheltered housing which was the Harveys' home. Driving past the entrance to it, Webb felt a twinge of guilt. He must get in touch with the old boy and put him in the picture as he'd promised.

The house they were now visiting was small and narrow, seemingly fitted in at a later date between two taller buildings. Mavis opened the door to them, a grey-haired woman in a floral dress, and ushered them ceremoniously into her front room. For the life of him, Webb could not connect her visually with the girl who had babysat for his parents.

'Mrs Parker, you probably don't remember me,' he began diffidently when they were all seated, and Jackson braced himself for another trek down memory lane. 'I'm Sheila's brother—David Webb.'

For a moment she stared at him blankly. 'Davy? You're Davy?'

He smiled. 'That's right.'

'Well, I'll go to the foot of our stairs! Fancy that now!'

'I've come, really, to test your memory of something that happened forty years ago.'

'Fire away!' she said confidently. 'There's not much I don't remember.'

'You'll have heard by now that Dick Vernon's been found?'

Her face clouded. 'I have indeed. What a shocking business, and so soon after Mr Makepeace, too.' She paused. 'Bit odd, it falling to you to look into it. What with the feud, I mean.'

'Yes, it's not too easy. Mrs Parker—'

'Oh, get away with you!' she interrupted. 'What's happened to "Mavis"?'

Just as long, thought Jackson stoically, as she doesn't keep calling the Governor "Davy".

'Very well, Mavis—thank you. I want you to think back to the day Mr Vernon disappeared.'

She nodded. 'I remember it as if it were yesterday.' And this, Webb thought with a tingle of excitement, would be an original statement. No one had apparently thought to question the girl at the time.

Without any prompting she launched into her story, but the detectives soon realized it would have to unfold at her own pace, interspersed with frequent reminiscences and comments.

'It was Sheila's birthday, her fifth. She was such a lovely little girl, wasn't she? I used to feel so proud when I took her for walks; I'd pretend she was mine. Well, like I said, it was her birthday and they were to have a picnic tea in Piper's Wood. I couldn't go, of course, because I was working—had a job at the dairy at the time.'

'The *dairy?*' Webb interrupted. 'Vernon's Dairy?'

'That's right.'

'Did my parents know?'

'They must have, but we never mentioned it. Anyway, because I couldn't go to the picnic, your mum said to pop round later and have a piece of cake and I could give Sheila her present then.'

'Do you know where my father was that evening?'

'He was there when I arrived—I made sure of that.'

Seeing Webb's puzzlement, she smiled. 'I've a confession to make, Chief Inspector. When I was sixteen, I was madly in love with your dad!'

Webb stared at her disbelievingly. 'You were?'

'Oh yes. Such a tall, strong, silent man—just like a film star.' This was indeed a new vision of his father. 'And how he loved that little girl! I used to watch them together from my bedroom window. I remember once, your dad had spent all afternoon planting out seedlings. Then Sheila trotted out and when he wasn't looking, pulled up about a dozen of them. I held my breath, I can tell you, when he turned round and saw what she'd done. I heard her piping little voice say, "Pretty flowers for Mummy," and after a moment he just laughed and picked her up and hugged her.' She shook her head, lost in her memories, and Webb found himself powerless to steer her back to the point.

'And the way he looked at your mum! Made my knees turn to water, I can tell you. Adored her, didn't he? I used to dream of having a man who'd look at me like that.'

Webb's thoughts whirled. Was it accurate, this entirely new picture of his father? Had jealousy and resentment blinded him to the true man? Perhaps he and Sheila had been wrong and John Webb really had fallen for Dick Vernon's fiancée. Whatever the ethics of his taking her from him, it might after all have been done out of love. Even more bitter, then, would be his realization that she did not and never would love him.

'Anyway,' Mavis was continuing, 'to get back to your question, yes, your dad was there when I arrived, but he went out soon after to his bowls. And when you two were in bed, your mum and me sat and chatted in the kitchen.'

'She hadn't asked you to sit for her?'

'No, but that's what I ended up doing, because she had a phone-call, didn't she?'

He'd wondered how they'd arranged to meet. 'Who was it, do you know?'

'She never said, but I thought at the time it was your dad.'

'Even though he'd just gone out?'

'It was something in her voice. Something—tender, like.'

Then there'd been blindness on Mavis's part too. Lilian Webb had never in her life addressed her husband with tenderness.

'Did you hear what she said?'

'Well, I was trying not to listen, like. But something about, "I know. Of course I know." And then she said, "Isn't it rather—" and I couldn't catch the next word.'

It was probably "risky", Webb thought caustically.

'Then she said, "All right, but I mustn't be long." And she came back into the kitchen with her cheeks all pink and asked if I could stay for an hour as she had to go out. So of course I did.'

'What time was this?'

'Half-eight,' she answered promptly.

'You're sure?'

'Positive. Frankie Howerd was on the wireless—there was no telly then—and I turned it on just as she went out.'

'And was she only an hour?'

'Less, but she got back in a terrible state, crying and shaking. Said she'd fallen over and hurt herself, but she wouldn't show me where. So when I was sure there was nothing I could do, I went home.'

'You didn't see my father come back?'

She shook her head. 'No. And it was the very next morning that Mr Vernon didn't turn up at the dairy, and there was such a kerfuffle going on, with Mrs Vernon in a fair state phoning the police and everything. And from that day no one saw hair nor hide of him till you dug him up yourself yesterday!'

She looked across at Webb's shell-shocked face, well pleased with herself. 'I told you there was nothing wrong with my memory,' she said proudly.

'I'd say it's photographic. It brought things back for me too.' He hesitated. 'Did my mother ever refer to that evening again?'

'No. I did ask if she was better the next day, but she

didn't want to talk about it. It must have shaken her up, though, because she was pale as a ghost for the rest of that week. Now, here I am quite carried away with myself, and not offering you a cup of tea! It'll only take a minute.'

She bustled out of the room. One glance at Webb's face made Jackson hold his tongue and the two men sat in silence until she returned with a tray. Somehow, a more or less one-way conversation was maintained while they drank their tea and then took their leave.

'People wondered, you know,' Mavis Parker confided, as she led them to the front door, 'at me marrying a man old enough to be my father. I'll tell you a secret, Davy Webb: I married Bert because he reminded me of your dad.'

CHAPTER 12

Webb filled in what remained of the afternoon in the office allocated to him at Silver Street, reading through the mass of reports which had accumulated on his desk. There were statements by an assortment of people who had known Billy Makepeace—his own farm workers, magistrates, members of the church. One or two, read together with the policeman's impressions of the interviewee, might stand further checking. One such was Stanley Fox, the church treasurer, who, Bob Dawson had noted, seemed on edge and unduly defensive. A finger in the collection plate, perhaps. Could Billy have been blackmailing him? It didn't seem in character.

At five-thirty Jackson knocked and looked round the door. 'Will you be wanting me at the Vernons', Guv?'

'No, Ken, I don't expect to get much, it's more a case of garnering impressions. We have their statements on Makepeace, and they were only kids when their father died.' He paused, thinking of Rona Vernon and her self-conscious flush at the graveside. He'd like to get to the bottom of that.

'All right if I go home, then? I can get a lift back with the lads.'

'Yep. I shan't be far behind you; I intend to sleep in my own bed tonight. Meet me at Carrington Street in the morning.'

There was still the question-mark raised by Colin's non-attendance at the Dinner, Webb reflected as the door closed behind Jackson, but he'd seen enough of his family for the moment. That would keep till tomorrow.

Tom Vernon and his wife lived in the old family home from which Dick had gone out to meet his death. It was in a winding cul-de-sac of large, detached houses off the Broad-minster road into town. Having parked his car at the gate, Webb walked to the bottom of the road which ended, as it always had, in a wooden gate giving on to fields. He stood for a moment, the evening sun in his eyes, staring out across the grass to the boundary wall of the cemetery in Chapel Lane.

Dick must have come this way that last evening, crossed the fields to Chapel Lane, skirted Piper's Wood to reach the Heatherton Road, then over the style into the field in which the old barn stood. It wouldn't have taken him more than ten minutes, going cross-country like that.

It troubled Webb that he alone knew where Dick had been that evening and whom he had met; knowledge that was vital now murder was involved. And he was again brought up against the unpalatable fact that the only person who seemed to have a motive was his own father, with whom Dick had had a fight on the night of his death. A fight, moreover, which had left him at the very least uncon-scious on the barn floor.

Alone in the deserted road, Webb agonized over whether he was justified in holding back that knowledge for a few more days. Naturally, should any more definite suspicion present itself he would go straight to Fleming, lay the facts before him and ask once again to be relieved of the case. Failing any such development, though, a day or two's grace was surely not much to ask before laying his father open to a posthumous charge of, at best, manslaughter.

He turned and slowly retraced his steps to the Vernon house. They were all assembled to meet him, united against a common foe. Which was something he had to break up for a start.

'Good evening,' he began pleasantly. 'Thank you for agreeing to see me.'

'You mean we'd a choice?' Larry muttered sourly.

'I'm not sure whether you realize,' Webb continued, 'but we're working on the assumption that your father's death and that of Mr Makepeace were in some way linked.'

That surprised them as much as it had Jenny Hawthorn. 'How do you make that out?' Tom demanded. He was smoking a cheroot, and the hazy smoke from it melded into a shaft of sunlight, masking his face.

'We have our reasons,' Webb returned smoothly. 'My intention in coming here is to probe your memories again of the nights when both men died, and see if we can establish any more definite links. And to do that—' his eyes went from one closed face to another—'it will be necessary to see you separately.'

'But that'll take the whole bloody evening!'

'I doubt it, sir. So, if there's a room we could use for the interviews, we can make a start.'

Rona Vernon rose to her feet. 'I'll show you to the study,' she said.

'Thank you. By the way, since my sergeant isn't here to take notes, I've brought a tape-recorder. I presume no one has any objection?'

Again his bland eyes surveyed them in turn, and although there was some muttering among the men, no one objected. 'Good. Then I'd like to see the gentlemen first, please.' Rona was waiting by the door, and Webb followed her across the hall to a smaller room dominated by a large desk.

'Thank you, this will do admirably.'

She smiled perfunctorily, not looking at him. 'I'll send my husband in,' she said.

Tom Vernon plonked himself down in an easy chair and

stared defiantly at Webb, who had seated himself behind the desk. Webb switched on the machine and went through the standard preliminaries.

'Mr Vernon, what do you remember of the day your father disappeared?'

'I don't think I saw him at all. He hadn't come down by the time we left for school, and afterwards we went to Colin Fairchild's for tea. Then we came home and went to bed.'

'It was the day after your aunt's funeral,' Webb reminded him.

'I know that,' Tom said testily, drawing on his cigar, 'but I presume it's personal memories you're after? What I'm saying is that Larry and I were aware of very little at the time, but the events of that day have been gone over so often and in so much detail that it's hard to separate what we actually saw from what we heard about later.'

'Such as what?'

Vernon shrugged. 'Dad was hovering on the brink of a breakdown—not hearing when people spoke to him, withdrawing more and more into himself. And he'd always been such an outgoing person. There were business worries too, but they were as nothing compared to the trauma of his sister's death. All this I know now, but I doubt if I realized more than a fraction at the time.'

'What exactly *did* you realize?'

'We were aware something was going on, and we weren't above listening at doors, but it didn't make us much the wiser. All we really gathered was that Dad hadn't just gone away for a few days, as we'd been told.'

He leant forward to stub out his cigar. Its pungent aroma scorched Webb's nostrils and he surreptitiously moved the ashtray to the edge of the desk.

'Everyone assumed he'd lost his memory,' Tom continued, seeming now to be thinking aloud. 'Certainly he'd been under enough stress. It was an odd set-up, you know, between him and Aunt Joan. He was closer to her than he was to Ma, and not unnaturally Ma resented it.' He uncrossed his legs, seeming suddenly to realize in whom he'd been confiding and resenting the fact. 'Well, there you have it. I can't think it's going to be much good to you.'

'You haven't remembered anything further about last Monday?'

'No, I haven't.'

'Very well, Mr Vernon. Thank you. Would you ask your brother to come in, please?'

Larry told much the same story as his twin—hardly surprising, since as children they'd done everything together. He did remember hearing talk about various sightings, and confessed that for some months he'd tried to believe his father would return. Like his brother, he could offer nothing new on the previous week when Makepeace had met his death.

Following Larry, his wife, Frances, came hesitantly into the room. She was pale, fair, and, Webb had thought, nondescript, but away from her sister-in-law, whose vivid colouring accentuated her pallor, she had a certain quiet charm. 'I really don't see how I can help you, Chief Inspector,' she began. 'I never knew my father-in-law, nor had I anything to do with Mr Makepeace. As you're aware, there was bad feeling between the families.'

'Where were you on the evening he died, Mrs Vernon?'

'At the WI meeting.'

No alibi for her husband, then. 'What time did you get home?'

'About a quarter to eleven, I suppose.'

'Was your husband in?'

'No, he'd gone to the cricket match.'

'So what time did he get back?'

'Soon afterwards. We sat downstairs for a few minutes and discussed our respective evenings before going to bed.' There was little else she could tell him, and he released her to go and send Rona.

It was clear at once that she was ill at ease. She glanced apprehensively at the machine whirring softly on the desk before sitting down, knees close together and hands clasped.

Hoping to make her relax, Webb said with a smile, 'It seems a long time since tennis club days.'

She looked up then, and he was struck again by her beauty, the high cheekbones, arched brows and unusual eyes, the vibrant, fashionably cut hair. In his jaundiced opinion, they were wasted on Tom Vernon.

Slowly she smiled. 'Yes, I remember. You were at Shillingham Grammar, weren't you?'

'And you were at St Anne's.' Webb moved the silver inkwell an inch to the right. 'You were sixteen or so when you arrived in the district. Was Dick Vernon's disappearance still talked about?'

'When I started going out with Tom, people went out of their way to tell me about it.'

'What was the general opinion?'

'That he'd wandered off with amnesia and was probably dead.'

'Did Tom mention him?'

'Not till I asked, but he couldn't tell me anything more.'

'What about the Makepeaces?'

She jerked as though a nerve had been prodded. Then she said quickly, 'I knew Jenny before Tom and I were engaged. Frankly, I resented being forced into that ridiculous feud. I considered it puerile, and I still do.'

'You knew the old man?'

Her colour deepened. 'Only vaguely.'

'Where were you, Mrs Vernon, the night he died?'

She glanced almost fearfully at the tape-recorder. 'In Oxbury, at the cinema.'

He raised an eyebrow. 'Who with?'

'By myself.' Her cheeks were burning now. 'There was a film I particularly wanted to see, and that was my only free evening. My husband couldn't come because he'd arranged to meet some friends.'

Webb sat looking at her, his fingers slowly turning the inkwell. Not true, he thought. Definitely not true. Where had she really been?

'Is there anything else you'd like to say?'

'No,' she said, breathing fast.

'That's all, then.'

She rose quickly. 'You're coming back to the sitting-room?'

'In a moment.'

'Very well.' She paused with her hand on the door knob. Then she said softly, 'Thank you' and was gone.

Webb stared at the closed door. What had she thanked him for? Not persisting in his questioning? Avoiding subjects that would have embarrassed her? He reached for the machine, rewound it for a second or two, then pressed the play button. His voice said 'In a moment,' and hers replied 'Very well.' He bent forward, listening intently, but all he heard was the closing of the door. Her soft 'Thank you' had not registered on the recorder, as, no doubt, she'd intended.

He switched it off and sat back, turning over in his mind the questions and answers that had been made. Then, with a sigh, he stood up and went to bid his reluctant hosts good night.

Outside on the pavement again, Webb hesitated. He had known when this case started that sooner or later he would have to visit the old barn and exorcise the hold it had on him. Now seemed as good a time as any, and at the same time he could re-enact Dick Vernon's movements that night. Perhaps it would give some idea as to what had happened.

Accordingly he walked back to the gate at the end of the road, and with some difficulty managed to slide back the rusty bolt and let himself through into the field. It was full of wheat, waist-high now and rippling in the slight breeze, but a public right of way lay alongside the hedge and down this Webb walked in the evening sunshine, as had Dick Vernon all those years ago. Over to his right he could see the cemetery wall. Dick could little have realized that he would end the night within its confines. Perhaps, in his mental torment, he would not have cared.

Another gate at the far side of the field gave access to

Chapel Lane. As though performing some kind of rite, Webb went through it, crossed the narrow road, and entered the field alongside the copse which, in his youth, had been known as Piper's Meadow. Now, it was given over to potatoes. His countryman's eyes approved the healthy crop as he followed the path to the busy Heatherton road where he had to wait a moment or two before crossing.

And now, pausing on top of the stile, he could see the old barn. Owned by Red Roofs Farm down the road, it had fallen into disuse years ago, but the farmer left it standing as sanctuary for the barn-owls which nested there. In its solitary splendour it had long been a local landmark.

From his vantage-point, Webb looked around him. At his back the cars continued to roar past, but ahead of him the countryside lay more or less as it had for centuries, grass and hedgerows and birdsong in the evening air, larches and oaks heavy with summer foliage. Beneath him buttercups, daisies and scarlet poppies made a painter's palette of the grass. He drew a deep breath and vaulted down from the stile.

How had Dick felt as he entered this field forty years ago? What thoughts were going round his head as he hurried to meet his erstwhile sweetheart, and what had made this meeting so imperative? Having lost his sister, did he intend to ask Lilian to run away with him? Was that what John Webb had interrupted?

And now he'd reached the barn and his nostrils picked up the faint, well-remembered scent of sun-warmed creosote. He glanced at his watch. Nine minutes since he'd left the Vernons' gate. Dick had left home about eight-thirty, Mrs Vernon said, which tied in with Mavis's recollection of his phone-call. He would have arrived here, then, at much the same time as Lilian. They could not have had long together before John Webb arrived.

What had alerted him to the rendezvous? The bowling green was in Bridge Street, almost parallel with the barn and some half-mile away. Perhaps, looking up from his game, he had seen the bright colour of her dress as she crossed the field to the barn.

Webb studied the outside stair leading to the hay loft, up which he had crept to spy on Beth Jones. The wooden steps were rotten, some of them missing and the rest hanging loose. Better not attempt to climb them. Instead he walked round to the door of the barn, which was hanging loosely from one hinge. He pushed it open and stepped inside.

He had not been in this building since the night his father struck down Dick Vernon, but over the years it had troubled his dreams. Though not as large as he remembered, it was imposing enough with its vaulted roof and the hayloft at one end. He advanced across the floor, the sepia shadow of his boyhood keeping pace with him as memories crowded in, of picnic teas in the early days, of schoolboy gang-meetings on long summer afternoons. A rusty old plough stood in one corner, with a pile of straw in front of it. Dotted around, too, were more modern arte-facts, the ubiquitous drinks cans and empty crisp packets. Doubtless today's young lovers also met here.

He looked up at the roof and to his delight was able to distinguish the humped, feathery forms of a couple of owls at the far end of one beam. He hoped he was not disturbing them. His eyes moved along to the trapdoor, closed now, and suddenly, intensely, his sensations as he had lain up there came back to him, mouth dry and heart pounding at the sound of his father's voice. If only he could remember the entire conversation!

As he had instructed Sheila outside the cemetery, Webb closed his eyes and willed himself back into the past—the warm hay pricking his bare legs, the dusty smell of it. But strive as he would, the initial words remained elusive and he could recall only those he'd repeated to Hannah, ending with Dick's frantic "I *had* to see her, I needed—' and then the punch that silenced him.

Webb opened his eyes on the present. *Why* had it been so important for Dick to see Lilian that night? If John had held his temper, he might have explained. Perhaps it had not been an amorous assignment, but a consultation, a plea for advice on a course of action? But what? And had it anything to do with Dick's death?

THINK! he commanded himself. Assuming, because he must, that his father had not killed Dick, what possible reason would anyone else have to do so? On all sides, he had been assured of Dick's popularity and easygoing nature. The photograph on his widow's piano bore that out.

Billy Makepeace was an obvious suspect. General opinion was that he and Dick had had no contact for years —but the same had been assumed of his father. Perhaps some more recent enmity had blown up between them, too. According to his statement, Billy had spent that evening at home with his family, a fact corroborated by his wife. Had there been real grounds for suspicion, that alibi would not have counted for much.

Or what of Eileen Vernon? She was a strong-minded woman and had resented her sister-in-law's influence. Suppose she'd followed Dick when he left the house that evening, had witnessed his meeting with Lilian? No, Webb decided, it wasn't feasible. Even if she could have brought herself to kill her husband, she would have been incapable of reopening the grave and burying him. Unless, of course, she had help. But again, who?

He sat down on the pile of straw and reviewed the position. If his father's blow hadn't killed him, Dick must at some stage have come round. What would he have done? The obvious answer, surely, was to set out for home. So who had prevented him reaching it? Someone who had known where to find him that evening—which was extremely unlikely—or someone he'd met by chance? And why should a chance meeting have such disastrous consequences?

Webb sat on, plunged in thought, while the shadows outside grew longer and the interior of the barn dimmer. If Dick had met someone on his way home, it was more likely to be as he crossed one of the roads rather than in the fields.

But why had whoever it was suddenly turned on him and struck him down, this time fatally? It didn't make sense.

A faint sound of voices impinged on his senses and for a moment, still enmeshed in the past, the hairs rose on the back of his neck. Then a girl's laugh sounded nearer at hand, and a young couple, arms twined round each other, appeared in the doorway. They were inside the barn before they saw Webb, and as he rose from his pile of straw the girl gave a little scream.

'Sorry!' he said quickly. 'It's all right, I'm just going.' And he passed them hastily and started back across the field, aware of them staring after him. He hoped their tryst would have happier consequences than the one he'd just reconstructed.

Minutes later he was edging his car out of the cul-de-sac where the Vernons lived on to the main road. It was then he noticed the pub on the corner, where Dick had mentioned going for cigarettes that last evening. On an impulse he pulled into its car park and went inside.

As he had hoped, it was filled to capacity, everyone laughing and talking at the same time. He ordered half a pint of bitter and felt the tensions inside him begin to ease. This impersonal friendliness was the perfect antidote to the haunted shadows of the barn. He had revisited his boyhood that evening; it had not been an easy exercise, nor, as far as he could see, had it achieved anything. But tomorrow was another day.

Colin said, 'Oh, there you are. What are you doing in the dark?'

Sheila turned, blinking as he switched the light on and the twilit garden disappeared into a reflection of the room behind her.

'Thinking,' she said.

He walked over and sat in the easy chair opposite. 'What about?'

'All kinds of things. You, me, David, Mr Makepeace, Dick Vernon.'

'Did you reach any conclusions?'

'A few. We've been forced to take stock of ourselves this past week, and I'm not sure I like what I see.'

Colin was watching her warily. 'In what respect?'

'For one thing, I've had to think more deeply about my parents; particularly since David had me reliving that ghost business. And I found it all rather depressing.'

He sighed. 'Yes.'

'I didn't tell you before, but I can't see why you shouldn't know. Mum was once engaged to Dick Vernon.'

'My God! How long have you known that?'

'Since she was dying. I told David the other evening. What's more, I don't think they ever stopped loving each other.'

'Well, that would explain your father's attitude.'

'And hers,' Sheila said defensively. 'He took her away from Dick, after all. They would probably have been very happy together.'

'She made her choice.'

'But it was the wrong one. They were never happy, were they? Not that I remember.' She paused and added reflectively, 'I was so determined my marriage would be better than theirs.'

'And isn't it?' he asked quietly.

'Until last week I'd have said it was. Now I'm not so sure. It's different, certainly.'

He stood up and went over to the drinks table, where he poured two whiskies. 'Why the qualification?' he asked, handing her one of the glasses.

She looked up, her eyes challenging him. 'What do you think? Would you say we have a successful marriage?'

He smiled crookedly. 'I need warning of a question like that.'

'You shouldn't,' she said seriously. 'When you gave up university and we bought this place, I was determined to be at your side every step of the way, an equal partner.'

'But,' he suggested, 'you've ended up a bit more equal than I am?'

She met his eye. 'That's what I was wondering. Or rather, I wondered if that's what you thought. Perhaps you've answered my question.'

He said gently, 'Sheila, I've always been grateful for your support, you know that. You also know that it's long been my opinion that you drive yourself too hard. I understand the reason for it—I think you do, too. Perhaps now it's even more apparent.'

'And somewhere along the way we've lost something?'

'Perhaps.'

'No wonder I'm feeling depressed.'

'Look, we have a lovely home, a successful business, two fine healthy children—'

'Yes, yes, I know. We've a lot to be thankful for, but are we happy? Are we really any happier than my parents were? Or are we two separate people happening to live under the same roof, as they were?'

He was silent, staring down into his glass. She watched him for a minute or two. Then she said, 'Do you love me, Colin?'

He looked up quickly. 'What kind of question is that?'

'Do you?'

'Of course I do.'

'Honestly?'

'Honestly.'

She sighed. 'I suppose that's all right, then,' she said.

CHAPTER 13

The next morning Webb put in a couple of hours at his own desk before setting out for Erlesborough. They'd woken to heavy rain—the first in weeks—and now, sitting beside Jackson in the car, he watched the rhythmic sweeping of the windscreen wipers and reflected that the change in the weather would suit Colin. Last week's brief thunderstorm had barely penetrated the soil; this steady soaking should provide badly needed moisture.

His brother-in-law had come naturally into his mind because he was on his way to see him, and not looking forward to the encounter. He did not seriously suspect Colin of killing Makepeace, but if he had nothing to hide, why lie about the Old Boys' Dinner? Whatever the reason, he had to uncover it, even if it marred their relationship for evermore. That was one of the hazards of his profession.

'Won't be much fun trailing around in this,' Jackson said gloomily, as a lorry overtook them sending a deluge of dirty water over the car.

'Fun isn't the name of the game, lad,' Webb rejoined. 'At least be thankful it stayed dry for the exhumation.'

Jackson grunted. 'Where are we making for specifically?'

'You can drop me off at The Old Farmhouse; I have to tackle my brother-in-law about his alibi, but it would be politic to do so privately. In the meantime there are still a few magistrates to track down; there's just a chance they might know of some villain with a grudge against Billy. See what you come up with, and we can compare notes over lunch. Not the Narrow Boat today, I think; it'll be dreary down by the canal in this weather. Let's try the Fox and Grapes in Bridge Street. I'll walk back and meet you there in an hour's time.'

Sheila opened the door to him, and Webb thought how tired she was looking.

'Come in,' she said. 'Time for a coffee?'

'I can make time.' He followed her to the kitchen. The cat was crying at the back door and when Sheila let it in, rain blew into the room on a gust of wind. The cat rubbed its wet fur against her legs and she pushed it away.

'I know we need rain,' she commented, 'but it does complicate things. I've some bedspreads waiting to be hung out, but not a chance today.'

'Colin around?' Webb asked casually, seating himself at the table.

'He's deadheading houseplants. Do you want him?'

'I'd like a word, when we've had coffee.' He watched her pour boiling water on to the grounds. 'I went to see Mavis, by the way.'

Sheila turned quickly. 'Oh yes? How did you get on?'

'She has a fantastic memory but it wasn't really much help. She was there, though, when Dick phoned, which ties up that loose end.'

'She knew it was him?'

'No, no. She thought it was Father, for some reason.' He paused. 'Did you know she had a crush on him?'

'On Dad? But she was only a kid.'

'None the less, she worshipped him from afar. What was more, she commented on how fond of Mother he was.'

Sheila came slowly to the table with the coffee-pot.

'So,' Webb continued, looking up into her face, 'perhaps you wronged him in suspecting he only married her to spite Dick.'

'If so, I'm delighted. I was always fond of him, as you know, but since Mum told me about Dick and how Dad had muscled in on them, I've not felt the same.'

'To get back to that evening, Mavis says Mother was very upset when she came home. She pretended she'd fallen and hurt herself, but Mavis wasn't convinced.'

Sheila poured the coffee. 'I've remembered something else too, though I don't suppose it's important.'

'Tell me anyway.'

'It must have been that week or the following one. In the very early days of my nightmares, anyway. I woke up after a bad dream and ran out on the landing, intending to go to Mum and Dad's room for comfort. But then I heard them shouting at each other. Mum screamed, "What did you do to him?" and Dad shouted back, "What did you?" I was frightened to go in, and crept back to bed.' She shuddered. 'David, you don't really think he killed Dick Vernon, do you?'

'No,' he said, hoping he spoke the truth, 'but I have to prove he didn't.' He stirred his coffee reflectively. His sister had been frank with him; he owed her the same courtesy.

'Sheila, there's something I didn't tell you about that night.'

She tensed, nerving herself for what was to come. 'Well?'

'I did go to spy on the courting couple, as I said. And I fell asleep as I said. But I was woken by shouting voices, and I peered through the trapdoor to see Father and Dick confronting each other.'

She had whitened. 'David, you didn't see Dad—?'

'I saw him knock Dick down. Then he stormed off. I waited for quite a while, but Dick hadn't stirred by the time I crept away and ran home.'

She made a soft, moaning sound. Then she whispered, 'So you were the last person to see him alive?'

'The *next* to last, I hope.'

Sheila lifted her cup with fingers that shook. 'And you've kept that secret all these years?'

He nodded.

'It explains a lot of things,' she said quietly. She looked up, meeting his brooding eyes. 'What are you going to do?'

He shrugged. 'I should have gone to the Chief Super as soon as his skeleton was identified. I'm breaking all the rules, but I've given myself another forty-eight hours to try to clear Father.'

She put a hand on his. 'Thank you.'

'I might see things more clearly when I set them down,' he continued. Webb's habit of illustrating his cases was well-known at Carrington Street, where it was referred to as 'drawing conclusions'. Often, sketching out the background to a case and inserting cartoon figures of the suspects pointed him in the direction of a murderer. The need to draw was building inside him, but his equipment was at home.

'I can provide pencil and paper.'

'Oh, I'll probably last till this evening.' On the other hand, the sooner he got down to it, the better; once the need established itself, it was not easy to hold off. He looked at her with a smile. 'If I change my mind, though, I might pop back this afternoon. Would that be OK?' Provided, he told himself, Colin hadn't by that time barred him from the house.

He finished his coffee and stood up. 'In the meantime I must get on. I'll just go and have a quick word with Colin.'

'He's in the houseplant greenhouse—it's the nearest one to the house. Have you got an umbrella?'

'No, I can't be bothered with them. I'll just make a dash for it.'

She opened the back door for him and then, to his surprise, reached up and kissed his cheek. 'Good luck,' she said.

Colin was indeed engaged in deadheading, moving slowly along the displays with a pair of secateurs in his hand. He stopped when he saw Webb enter the greenhouse and stood waiting for him to approach. There were a few people wandering around—probably come in out of the rain, Webb thought—but they were at the far end and would be unable to hear their conversation.

As Webb came up, Colin said flatly, 'I've been expecting you. Have you seen Sheila?'

'Yes, I've just had coffee with her.'

'Did you tell her why you're here?'

'Only that I needed a word with you.'

'Thanks.'

The second time he'd been thanked by his family in the space of five minutes. Webb ran a variegated leaf gently between finger and thumb. 'Are you going to tell me where you were last Monday?'

'Not murdering Billy Makepeace.'

'Colin, I need to know.'

'Yes.' He sighed deeply. 'This is not going to be easy, David.'

There was a brief pause. A low hum of voices came from the browsers at the far end of the greenhouse. Outside, rain cascaded down the panes and made a steady pattering on the glass roof above them. Webb waited patiently.

Colin stirred and squared his shoulders. 'It would be hard enough telling anyone, let alone you.'

'Another woman?'

Colin looked at him sharply, then nodded.

'Rona Vernon, by any chance?'

His brother-in-law looked startled. 'How the hell did you know that?'

'I saw her yesterday. I think she thought I knew.' Which was why she, too, had thanked him.

'Sheila and I haven't been close for some time. I don't know whether you've noticed during your Christmas visits.' To his shame, he hadn't. 'And Rona and I had a thing going years ago, before either of us was engaged. It just—suddenly flared up again.'

Colin snapped savagely at a stem and a lovely, overblown hibiscus bloom fell to the floor at their feet. 'I suppose it's useless saying I didn't mean to hurt Sheila. It's true, though. But she didn't seem to need me any more. She's so all-fired efficient and highly motivated, she doesn't need *anyone*. At least, that was how it seemed. After last night, I'm not so sure.'

Webb waited for an explanation of last night, but it wasn't forthcoming. 'And Monday?'

'That was just bloody bad timing. In fact, Billy Makepeace had seen us together the previous week. We always met well away from Erlesborough, so you can imagine our horror when he walked into a pub in Popplewell. Popplewell, I ask you!'

Webb had to smile. The tiny village outside Steeple Bayliss must certainly have seemed a safe haven. 'Did he speak to you?'

'No, just stared. Then a knowing smile spread over his face. We were so unnerved we left straight away. But the incident made us stop and think. Suppose Billy, who had no love for our respective families, broadcast the news? How would we feel if Sheila and Tom found out about us? I think we both realized our homes and families meant more to us than we did to each other. So we arranged to

meet one last time, really just to end it. And as luck would
have it, it was the night Billy got himself murdered.'

'Where did you meet that time?'

'A hotel the far side of Oxbury. We'd—used it before.
The manager would confirm it.' Colin stared down at the
collapsed bloom on the floor. 'You can't have a very high
opinion of me. I haven't of myself. But I do love Sheila,
David. I realized last night, when she asked me outright. I
think now this ghost business has been explained she's been
doing a bit of self-analysis. She realizes we've drifted apart,
and we've a good chance of coming close again. That is, if
she doesn't find out about Rona. There's no point in telling
her, is there, since it's over?'

'No, I agree. Salving your conscience with a confession
would do more harm than good.'

'I feel pretty rotten, you know. There's nothing I
wouldn't do to make it up to her.'

Webb smiled. 'Don't overdo it, or you'll arouse her suspicions. I hope things work out.'

Colin smiled wryly, rousing himself from his preoccu-
pations. 'How's the case going, anyway? Any progress on
Dick's death?'

'With the trail stone cold it's not easy. I'm banking on a
link with Billy.'

'And it's Sheila's ghost story?'

'I think it has to be. If we could only discover who Billy
told about it, we'd be home and dry. He must have called
on someone on his way to the club.'

'Nobody saw him?'

'If they did, they're not saying. It's so frustrating, Colin
—all kinds of permutations are floating round my head but
I can't pin them down. I need to set out what we've got in
black and white, as I was saying to Sheila. She's offered to
supply pen and paper if I get desperate.'

'We might see you later, then.'

Webb nodded. 'In the meantime I'll be on my way.'

Colin wiped his hand on his trousers and held it out.
Webb solemnly shook it. Both men knew their friendship

had been tested and seemed to have survived. Which, in the circumstances, was something to be thankful for.

Webb turned up his collar and set off in the rain, not, this time, along the towpath, which today would be a sea of mud, but down the main road. There was a continuous stream of traffic, and several times he had to dodge sprays of water which heavy wheels sent sluicing over the pavement. And still the rain fell relentlessly, darkening stone walls and dripping steadily through the heavy foliage overhanging the footpath, so that every so often an extra shower of drops landed on Webb's unprotected head.

Hands deep in his pockets, he scarcely noticed them. His mind was still on Colin and the effect the affair must have had on his marriage. He'd learned a lot about his family as well as himself during this investigation; provided he could clear his father and bring the case to a satisfactory conclusion, he and Sheila might finally be free of the past and able to get on with their lives.

Jackson was waiting for him at a corner table in the Fox and Grapes. Webb smoothed the excess water from his hair and hung his dripping raincoat on the stand. Jackson, who had watched him from across the room, grinned as he approached and sat down.

'Swim here, did you, Guv? You should have phoned and I'd have come for you.'

'A little bit of rain never hurt anyone,' Webb said stoically. 'And it's great for clearing the head.'

'You've solved the case, then?'

'No call to be cheeky. No, I haven't, but things are becoming clearer. I cracked Fairchild's alibi, by the way. He'd been indulging in a bit of hanky-panky on the side.'

'Couldn't have been easy telling you that.'

Webb took a long drink from the pint awaiting him. 'How did you get on? Any more leads?'

'The names of several villains who thought they got a raw deal from Makepeace, but if you ask me it's pretty thin.

A lad might swear vengeance when he's sentenced, but he usually calms down pretty quickly.'

Webb nodded. 'I'm going to take a couple of hours off, Ken, and try to map it all out. My sister will provide the wherewithal. In the meantime, I've a bit more checking for you.' He paused, wondering how to disclose Dick's presence in the barn while concealing his own and his father's.

'Remember Sam Wainwright saying my mother and Dick had been engaged?'

Jackson nodded warily.

'And Mavis told us she went out that evening after a phone-call? Well, I'm pretty certain it was Dick who phoned, asking her to meet him at the old barn.' He paused again, hoping Jackson wouldn't question the source of this unsubstantiated allegation. 'We know my mother arrived home, very upset, soon after nine. What we don't know is where Dick went from there.'

Jackson moved uneasily. He did wish the Governor's family wouldn't keep intruding into the case. And where'd he got this idea about a barn? It sounded pretty far-fetched to him; perhaps he wasn't being told the whole story.

He said cautiously, 'So you're saying that instead of going to the pub for cigarettes, Vernon went to this barn to meet your mum? Where exactly is it, Guv?'

'Almost directly opposite here, in the field bordered by Bridge Street and the Heatherton road. It's pretty derelict now, but it was a popular meeting place in my youth. I went there last night after seeing the Vernons. They still live in the same house, so I took the cross-country route as Dick would have done.'

Jackson was still looking sceptical, but to Webb's relief made no comment. 'He was in a state about his sister,' he continued, 'and, as my mother'd been upset, probably worried about her, too. Surely when he left the barn, the obvious place he'd make for was home. So why didn't he get there?'

'He'd have gone across the fields, you said?'

'That's the quickest way to his house. But he'd have had

to cross two roads, the Heatherton road and Chapel Lane.'

'Couldn't have been run over, could he, Guv?' Jackson asked hopefully.

'Stapleton says not. But if he bumped into someone—as he must have done, I reckon—it's more likely to have been on one of those roads than in the fields.'

'Unless someone saw him leave the barn and followed him?' Jackson suggested, which was a possibility Webb preferred not to consider.

'True. Still, let's take the roads first. It's forty years too late to try contacting motorists who'd used them that night, but some of the houses might still have the same occupants. So while I'm at my scribbling, I'd like you to round up a couple of the lads and do a house-to-house along both roads. Not the whole length of them, just the houses nearest to the access to the fields, where Dick would have crossed over. There won't be that many.'

Jackson nodded. 'Right you are, Guv. Now, what are we going to eat? I was looking at that blackboard before you arrived, and the grilled ham sounds tasty.'

Webb smiled. The preliminaries over, Ken was now ready to get down to the serious business. 'Make it two hams,' he said.

Knowing he'd want to be alone, Sheila had set up an old easel of Stephen's in the guest-room, and laid out a selection of pens, pencils and crayons and a large pad of paper.

Moses the cat was asleep on the bed, and she was about to shoo him off but Webb stopped her. 'He won't disturb me—might even bring me some luck. Heaven knows, I could do with it. Thanks, Sheila, this is perfect.'

'I'll leave you to it, then. Let me know if there's anything else you need.'

He nodded, already seating himself at the easel and reaching for the paper as he planned how to set about his task. Normally he sketched in the background first, the area in which the crime had taken place, but in the case of Dick Vernon the scene was not known. Almost without thinking, he embarked instead on a series of small pictures—a strip cartoon telling the story of that last day as far as he knew it.

In the first square he drew Dick, a caricature based on the portrait on the piano. He was shown locked in his bedroom staring at the wedding photo. Why did it have such a traumatic effect on him? There must have been other pictures of Joan about the house; was it just that it had been the last occasion they'd all been happy?

The next square was split in half—Dick making a phone-call, Lilian Webb—recognizable by her fair curls and down-turned mouth—receiving it. Then Dick's progress across the fields to the barn, and their meeting. One picture, drawn in more detail than the others, showed the loft above the barn, and the boy who lay asleep there. Webb stared at that square for a long time before, with a sigh, he forced himself to go on.

John Webb's arrival; Lilian's departure; the blow which felled Dick. That much was easy. But what next? How long had Dick lain there, and, when he finally came round—as, please God, he had—which way had he gone? Suppose, disorientated, he set off in the opposite direction from home? That would have taken him to the canal; might he have met Billy Makepeace there?

But guessing at this stage was against the rules; to be of any use, the drawings must keep to the facts as known. Perforce he left a gap, and the next square showed five-year-old Sheila and the figure in the graveyard. But what had happened in that blank space? Who had met Dick and killed him? And why?

Webb tore off the sheet and let it slide to the floor as he began to draw in more detail the possible actors in the drama. If one man were responsible for both murders, it was a pretty thin list of suspects. But he might be putting too much importance on that conversation in the café; Dick could just as easily have been killed by someone no longer alive, and Billy's murder have no connection with it.

There were therefore three groups to consider: those who

could have committed both crimes, and those who could have killed only Dick or only Billy.

Embarking on the first category, Webb began with Gus Lang the organist, who professed hardly to have known Dick but was a friend of Billy's. How true was either statement?

He considered the upright figure he had drawn, whose military bearing belied the sensitivity of his musical talents. A dual nature, to some extent; capable, therefore, of enmity as well as friendship? Webb doubted it, and moved on to Stanley Fox. Since he hadn't met the church treasurer a stick man had to suffice this time. Dawson'd suspected he was hiding something; perhaps he should go and see the man for himself.

In the meantime he turned to Dr Adams. He'd been around for both crimes but had hardly known Dick who, like his family, had been his partner's patient. And of Billy Makepeace he had spoken with affection.

The widow, then, Eileen Vernon? Webb sketched rapidly, considering the possibility. Strong-willed she certainly was, and determined, but not, he felt, murderous.

And Sam Wainwright: unhinged by grief, could he have resented Dick's being alive when his twin was dead? Hardly a believable motive, and he'd an alibi for Billy's death.

Which exhausted the first list. Webb leaned back in his chair and surveyed the representations of each in turn, trying to insinuate himself into their minds. What fears, guilts, secrets, lurked there? If there were any, they remained hidden from him.

Picking up his pen again, he was forced to admit that of those now dead who could have murdered Dick, the only likely suspects were his two old rivals, John Webb and Billy Makepeace. Carefully he drew in his father, surprised at how painful it proved. When he'd finished it—a few skilful lines bringing immediately to mind the dour, surly man who had dominated his childhood—he sat staring at it for a long time. Had John Webb loved his wife enough to kill his rival? Mavis Parker might have thought so.

So to Billy. The heavy face took shape beneath his pen
—broad, fleshy nose, thick neck and the aggressive, forward
thrust of the head. Had the old enmity between him and
Dick somehow rekindled, culminating in murder? If so,
there had been no hint of it.

Finally Webb turned to Billy's own murder, starting by
drawing the canal path with its railway bridge and the
steps up to Bridge Street. No mystery about this scene, but
precious few clues, either, he thought, sketching in the arch
of the bridge. Someone had lain in wait here—who was it?
Everyone knew of Billy's Monday ritual, the visit to the
club and the walk home along the towpath.

So to suspects relevant only to this case, the first of them
Jerry Croft. Had the old man nagged him once too often,
tipping his tightly controlled frustration over the edge into
violence? It was possible.

Then there was the solicitor, Martin Allerdyce, who'd
found the body. His likeness took shape on the page—
thinning hair, horn-rimmed spectacles. Makepeace was a
client of his; might he have been caught out in some mal-
practice?

Webb considered him and his statement for some time
before turning to the Vernon brothers. They had no love
for Billy; if they'd discovered something linking him with
their father's death, they might have turned violent. Yet
could a passion for revenge last all that time?

As with the other suspects, he thought dispiritedly, no
sooner did he divine a motive than common sense forced
him to discount it.

As he called these people to mind, most of whom he'd
known all his life, it occurred to Webb that this exercise,
no less than last night's visit to the barn, was part of his
exorcism of the past. During the last week he'd come to
realize that all his life he'd seen Erlesborough and everything connected with it through a distorting mirror. As he'd
gone about his inquiries his memories, both painful and
happy, had, against his will, been shaken up and fallen
back into a slightly different pattern. A split viewpoint had

been thrust before him, the memory of a child's impression melded with adult perception. It had forced him to re-examine, compare, contrast, and he now saw that nothing had been as clear-cut, as black and white, as he had supposed.

He looked again at his *dramatis personæ*. Billy, he was sure, had called on his murderer the night of his death. It had taken him an hour and ten minutes to reach the club instead of the usual twenty, leaving fifty minutes unaccounted for. A fair distance could be covered in that time, even by an elderly man unaccustomed to walking. In fact, depending on the time spent on the actual visit, most of the suspects' homes were within reach. No help from that angle.

Doggedly he went through the list again. Basically it was unlikely Billy would have approached the Vernons with his problem. Unlikely but not, Webb reminded himself, out of the question, since he'd already tried to contact Sheila that evening.

On the other hand Sam Wainwright, though related by marriage to the Vernons, had not been involved in the feud and, as Sam had indicated, the two men were on speaking terms. Therefore, if Billy thought he'd learned something pertaining to Dick's death, he was quite likely to call on the man's brother-in-law. But Sam had been playing whist— or so he said. He must check that the alibi had been verified.

Studying his little figures one after another, it struck Webb that one of Billy's most likely confidants would have been the man he considered an old friend—Dr Frank Adams.

He frowned, staring down at the caricature of the dapper little man with his moustache and the flower in his button-hole. He was known in the town as a devoted doctor, dedi-cated both to his profession and his patients, as Webb knew from Sheila's testimony. Though there'd been murderous doctors in the past, he found it hard to cast Frank Adams in the rôle. If he *had* killed Billy, it could only have been because he'd also murdered Dick. And Dick had died soon after Adams came to the area. What possible motive could he have had?

Webb sighed, trying to keep an open mind. No harm, anyway, in checking if Mrs Adams had been with her husband at the time Makepeace died. And as the thought came to him he recalled sitting in Janet Conway's pleasant sitting-room overlooking the fairway. How, he had asked, had she learned of Billy's death? From the doctor's wife, she'd replied, when she'd called to return the scarf *Vera left in the car after WI.*

So if Billy *had* called on him, Frank Adams would have been alone. But would he have had time—even if he wanted to—to lie in wait, push him in the canal, and still reach home before his wife?

And on cue Webb's memory again stirred. Sheila said she'd have phoned Billy back that evening, had she not been so late home. Had Vera been subjected to the same delay?

He pushed back his chair, strode to the door and hurried down the stairs, calling for his sister as he went. She came quickly into the hall to meet him, looking startled by his urgency.

'You were late home from WI last Monday?'

'That's right; old Mrs Simpson couldn't find her bag and had us all searching for it. Then, if you please, she remembered she hadn't brought it with her that evening.'

'How many of you stayed to look for it?'

'Angela, Janet and me. Oh, and Vera Adams, because Janet was giving her a lift.'

Webb let out his held breath. 'And you got home at what time?'

'After eleven-thirty. I thought Colin might have been back from his Dinner, but he wasn't. Why? Is it important?'

'It might very well be vital,' Webb said.

'But why? What possible—?' She was interrupted by the sudden strident ringing of the phone. She picked it up, then turned to Webb. 'It's for you, David. Sergeant Jackson.'

He almost snatched it from her. 'Ken? You've got something?'

'Yes, Guv, it looks like it. Best not over the phone, though.'

'How soon can you pick me up?'

'Five minutes?'

'I'll be ready.'

'Thanks, Sheila,' Webb said over his shoulder as he ran back up the stairs two at a time. He rapidly gathered up the sheets of discarded paper and stuffed them into his briefcase. Then, with a feeling of growing excitement, he raced back down the stairs and out to the gate to wait for Jackson.

CHAPTER 14

It had at last stopped raining, though as Webb stood waiting outside the Garden Centre he didn't register the fact. His brain was churning with the startling possibilities that had suddenly opened up, and he was impatient to learn whether Jackson's news would confirm or dispel them.

As the car drew up, he opened the door and slid into the passenger seat. 'What is it, Ken?'

'A bit of a shaker actually, Guv.'

'Dr Adams?'

Jackson's head spun round. 'How did you—?'

'Tell me.'

'Well, Bob took the Heatherton road and I did Chapel Lane. And I struck gold at the third house. A Miss Grant lives there—very nice lady, she is—head of English at St Anne's, she was telling me.'

'Go *on*, Ken.'

'I asked her if she'd always lived there, and she said yes, she was born there. So I explained what we were looking for, and asked whether she or her parents had happened to look out of the window that evening and see Dick Vernon.

I thought at first I'd drawn a blank, because she said no, she remembered the evening quite well because she'd been ill and certainly not looking out of any windows.

'But then she said that the reason she remembered it so clearly was because it was just after the first Mrs Wainwright's funeral, and everyone was in a state of shock over her death. She—Miss Grant, that is—was fifteen at the time—and she had German measles, too. No one had thought it was serious, but what with Mrs Wainwright dying, when her temperature suddenly shot up her parents panicked and phoned the doctor. And he in turn wouldn't have dared risk delaying his visit.

'And *then* she said, "Poor Dr Adams—he was only a young man then, still wet behind the ears." And I said— because that was what the doctor had told us—"He must have been glad Mrs Wainwright wasn't his patient." And she said, "No, but he'd been treating her, because Dr Nairn was away at a conference.'

Webb said slowly, 'Which was certainly not the impression he gave us.'

'That's what I thought, Guv. I didn't like to say too much, because I didn't want her thinking we were suspicious of the doctor, specially since I might have been off-beam anyway. But I did manage to get out of her that it was about half-nine when he went out to see her.'

'So he'd have left them just about the time Dick was returning from the barn.'

'I wondered about that, but if your mum got home at nine, wouldn't he have been earlier than that?'

Not if he was lying unconscious. 'He might have been glad of some time to himself. What I still don't understand, though, is what motive the doctor could have had for killing him. *If* he did.'

'Dick could have blamed him for his sister's death.'

'In the state he was in, quite probably. But Adams was a doctor, for heaven's sake. He'd have realized the man was still in shock.'

Jackson shrugged. 'Search me, Guv. So what do we do now?'

'I think, Ken, we'll go and have a word with Mr Harvey. I've felt guilty about not keeping in touch, and he might know something about the good doctor that we don't.'

George Harvey welcomed them eagerly and, when they were seated again in his little room with a tray of tea between them, listened attentively as Webb went through the case. When he reached that afternoon's disclosures, the old man's face grew grave.

'I don't like what I'm hearing, Chief Inspector. Frank Adams has been a good friend to us, along with the rest of the town. I don't fancy him in the guise of murderer.'

'Nor I, sir; but we have to consider the possibility, even though we've not come up with a plausible motive. I wondered if you'd any suggestions?'

'You read the earlier statements?'

'Yes, and I flicked through his again on the way here. He simply said he'd been calling on patients that evening. True, as we know, and no one tried to tie it down, because at the time it was thought Dick had just wandered off. More significantly, when asked for his opinion of Dick's state of mind, it was he who first mooted the amnesia theory.'

Harvey leant forward, hands clasped between his knees, and looked up at Webb from beneath bushy eyebrows. 'Are you proposing to go and charge him with it?'

'Not till I'm a lot more sure of my ground. We've no proof whatever at the moment, only a faint suspicion. What I do propose, though, is to go back and have another word with Mrs Vernon. There's something about that wedding photo that worries me. I wondered if you'd care to come with us?'

The old man brightened. 'That is good of you, my boy. I still feel the Vernon case is my baby, though I can't help hoping you're after the wrong bird.'

*

Mrs Vernon showed no surprise when the three of them arrived on her doorstep.

'Good afternoon, Mr Harvey—nice to see you again. I hope you're keeping well?'

'Very well, thank you, ma'am. A bad business about your husband. I'm very sorry.'

'Thank you. I think I was already resigned to it.' She turned to Webb, her face hardening. 'Well? What is it this time?'

'The wedding photo that arrived the day your husband disappeared. I'd be glad of some more details.'

'Whatever for?'

'I'm curious as to why it had such an effect on him.'

'It's simple enough, surely. Last family outing, and so on.'

'Have you by any chance still got it, Mrs Vernon?'

'Yes, as a matter of fact I have. Pure sentiment, really, but as I said, it was the last time—' She broke off and, rising, walked over to a walnut bureau which stood against the wall. When she turned back to him, Webb was surprised to see she was holding not the expected glossy photograph but a yellowing piece of newspaper.

'That was what came through the post?'

'Yes, a report from the local paper.'

'But you said it was a photograph.'

'So it is, Chief Inspector. Look.' She held out the paper and Webb took it, studying the faded wedding group and the typical local paper write-up describing the dresses of bride and bridesmaid. He'd been pinning his hopes on this photograph, but for the life of him he couldn't see anything significant in it.

'That's Joan,' Mrs Vernon said, pointing to a smiling woman standing on the right. 'You'd never have thought, looking at her, that she'd be dead within the week. And as it turns out, Dick soon after,' she added in a low voice.

So he'd been wrong. With a sense of anticlimax Webb flipped the paper over, running his eye down the item printed on the back. Then he stiffened. 'Mr Wainwright said the wedding was in Swansea?'

'That's right.' Mrs Vernon looked anxious. 'What is it? Have you found something?'

'The answer, perhaps, to two murders,' Webb said slowly. 'You told us earlier this arrived in the morning post, but you hid it from your husband.'

'That's right. I slipped it behind a cushion, meaning to destroy it later. But that evening he couldn't settle and he started wandering around plumping up cushions, and of course he found it.'

'You said he took it upstairs?'

'Yes, and when he came down he said he was going out for cigarettes.' Having made his phone-call to Lilian Webb, presumably. 'Why?' she added. 'What's wrong?'

He ignored her question. 'While you were in Wales, did any of you go off anywhere—a run in the country, perhaps?'

Puzzled, Mrs Vernon shook her head. 'Oh, apart from Joan. She went to tea with an old schoolfriend up the valley. They should have been at the wedding, but their little girl was ill.'

'Do you remember where they lived?'

'Goodness, I haven't thought of it in years. Pen-y-something.'

'Pen-y-Bryn?'

She gave a little exclamation. 'How did you know?'

'Mrs Vernon, I shall have to borrow this cutting. I'll take great care of it and it will be returned to you in due course.'

'But what's it all about?' she demanded. 'Aren't you going to explain?'

'Not at the moment, but I'll come back to you as soon as I can. Thank you for your cooperation.'

He was half way out of the room before Harvey and Jackson, startled and bewildered, struggled to their feet and followed him.

'And what the hell was all that about?' Harvey demanded explosively as they reached the privacy of the car.

Webb swivelled to face both men. 'On the back of this clipping is a report of an outbreak of meningitis in Pen-y-Bryn. Several people died before it was diagnosed.'

There was complete silence. After a moment he spoke into it, thinking aloud as he felt his way through the tragedy of forty years ago.

"It's my belief that it was that which killed Mrs Wainwright. And, unlike the encephalitis on her death certificate, it could have been treated if diagnosed in time.'

'So you were right,' Harvey said at last, just above a whisper.

'I imagine the symptoms are easily confused; especially by an overworked, inexperienced young man in the middle of a German measles epidemic. He'd have no reason to suspect meningitis.'

'And Dick Vernon, reading that, realized his sister might have been saved, and was after Adams's hide,' Jackson mused.

'We know there was no love lost between his wife and Joan, and, though shocked by her death, Mrs Vernon made it clear she resented the time he'd spent with her. So he decided to discuss the matter with my mother. But since I'm quite sure she never knew about it, they must have been interrupted before he got round to telling her. Perhaps,' Webb continued shamelessly, 'someone else came to the barn; it was a popular meeting-place for courting couples.' He no longer felt guilty about his half-truths. Beneath the surface, awaiting time for him to savour it, an enormous tide of relief was building up.

Harvey took up the story. 'So he set off for home, and as luck would have it, came upon Adams himself returning from visiting the Grant girl.'

Webb said quietly, 'I think it's time we called on the doctor and heard what he has to say.'

Dr Adams stood with his hand still on the door-knob, seeming to shrivel before their eyes. 'You'd better come in,' he said, adding to his wife, 'Vera, I'd like you to be in on this.'

'What is it, Frank?' Mrs Adams, who had appeared in the sitting-room doorway, looked startled by his tone. He did not reply. Sombrely he led the way into the study where they had spoken before and gestured to them to sit down. He himself remained standing, his back to the empty grate, as though facing his inquisitors. As, of course, he was.

Webb said quietly, 'Dr Adams, as you know, we're making inquiries into the deaths of Dick Vernon and Billy Makepeace. We think you might be able to help us.'

'Frank?' Mrs Adams's voice rose agitatedly, and she jumped up and went to stand beside her husband, taking his arm. He absent-mindedly patted her hand.

'What put you on to it?' he asked, almost conversationally.

'A number of things, but principally a cutting from a Welsh newspaper that arrived the day Dick disappeared. And, as we now know, died. Doctor, before we go any further I'm going to ask the sergeant here to caution you that—'

'Yes, yes, I think we can take that as read.'

'Wouldn't you prefer to sit down?' Webb suggested gently. With his wife still clutching his arm, the doctor moved to a couple of upright chairs and they both seated themselves.

'How much do you know?' he asked dully.

'That Mrs Wainwright was taken ill after visiting a village where there was an unsuspected outbreak of meningitis. And that Dick had just discovered the fact.'

He nodded. 'The symptoms are very similar—stiffness of the neck, nausea, vomiting. She even developed a rash, and I was too inexperienced and too geared to rubella to recognize it as the characteristic meningococcal rash. Her condition worsened rapidly, leading to coma and then death. I'd no hesitation at all in giving the cause as encephalitis following rubella.'

'And you met Dick that evening?'

'Yes. I'd been visiting Elizabeth Grant and had just got

into my car when I saw him come through the gate from Piper's Meadow. He stepped off the pavement, then, seeing the car, paused to let me pass. I thought he was drunk; he was swaying about with a dazed look on his face. Well, I was driving slowly and there was a full moon. As I drew level he recognized me.

'I lifted a hand as one does, but he suddenly darted forward and banged furiously on the car window. I stopped and opened the passenger door to see what he wanted, and was subjected to a barrage of verbal abuse such as I'd never heard before. I was astounded; I hardly knew the man, but he'd always appeared quiet and well-mannered. I put it down to drink, and it took me some time to realize he was accusing me of criminal negligence.

'Fortunately the road was deserted, but in case anyone came along I pulled him into the car, trying to calm him down until I could make out what he was getting at. As soon as I heard the word "meningitis" I knew. Everything clicked into place and I was panic-stricken. That rash— with hindsight it was obvious it hadn't been a rubella rash at all—I should have recognized it. And he was ranting on about reporting me to the medical council and having me struck off the register. I—I just lost my head.'

There was a silence. Vera Adams had started to weep quietly into her handkerchief.

The doctor roused himself from his traumatic memories. 'In mitigation, I might say I was almost dead on my feet. The rubella epidemic was at its height, my partner was away, and because it was the Whitsun holiday we'd been unable to obtain a locum. And since babies were being born and all the normal ailments continuing at their usual rate, I'd had only a couple of hours' sleep a night for the best part of a week.'

He paused, and added reflectively, 'Medicine had been my ambition for as long as I could remember. At long last I was qualified, in a good practice, and the world was my oyster. Then, out of the blue, this. Scarcely knowing what I was doing, I seized a spanner out of the glove compartment and lashed out at him. And he simply folded over in the car seat.'

He drew a deep breath. 'Well, we were only yards from the cemetery, and Joan Wainwright, as I knew only too well, had been buried the previous day. The ground would still be soft, and I kept a spade in the boot in case of snow in winter. It was almost too easy. The whole business was over in the space of an hour and before I'd emerged from my somnambulant state.'

No one spoke, and after a moment he continued. 'I checked, of course, about the Welsh outbreak, which confirmed both Vernon's accusation and my own fears. But it didn't take me long to realize that even if he had reported me, it wasn't likely any blame would be attached. And I mightn't have been able to save her, even with penicillin. In other words, if I hadn't panicked, if I'd just calmed him down and sent him home, it would probably all have blown over. But by the time I realized all this it was too late.'

Webb said inexorably, 'And what of Billy Makepeace? His death was deliberate and premeditated.'

The doctor wiped a shaking hand over his face. 'True; I wouldn't have believed myself capable of such action, but again I succumbed to panic.'

His wife had turned to him, her eyes widening. 'Mr Makepeace? Oh Frank, no!'

'He called round that evening soon after you'd gone out. He was full of some ghost-story Sheila Fairchild had been telling, which for some reason made him think she'd seen Vernon's murderer.' He looked at Webb almost accusingly. 'Perhaps you can explain?'

'My sister'd left a toy in Piper's Wood that afternoon. She woke in the night and set off to find it, and as she was passing the cemetery a figure rose up out of one of the graves. She had nightmares about it for years.'

'I see. It was shrewd of old Billy to work it out,' Adams said ruefully. 'Apparently he'd tried to ring both your sister for clarification and the vicar for advice, but both were out. So he came to me, poor devil.'

He looked up, wearily meeting Webb's eyes. 'And this time I *had* everything to lose; it wasn't a mistaken diagnosis I'd be accused of, but murder.'

'But he didn't suspect *you*, man!' old Harvey broke in. 'Why didn't you just fob him off, tell him it was nonsense? There was no need to *kill* him!'

'You know Billy. Once he had an idea in his head, he'd worry away at it till he got everyone else believing it too. I just couldn't take the risk. And when it came down to it, I suppose I felt my life here was of more value than his.'

He lifted his shoulders in a gesture of resignation. 'Actually, I hoped the shock of the cold water would do the trick with his heart condition, but he thrashed about so much I thought he was going to climb out.' He paused, then added expressionlessly, 'So I had to hold him down till it was over.'

Mrs Adams gave a strangled sob and ran stumblingly from the room. Her husband looked sadly after her.

'Not that it did me much good,' he continued. 'Billy wasn't the only one to put two and two together, and the exhumation took place.' He turned to Webb. 'So there you have it, Davy. Ironic, isn't it, that you should solve the murders of your father's two old rivals?'

Webb gestured to Jackson to read out the charge. Then he said flatly, 'If you'd like to pack an overnight bag, sir, we'll be getting back to Shillingham.'

It had been a painfully illuminating investigation, forcing Webb to re-examine himself, his conceptions and misconceptions, his beliefs, doubts and motivations. He said as much to Hannah over supper a few nights later.

'And I was damn lucky the gamble paid off,' he added. 'If it had turned out my father killed Dick, I could have been in trouble for withholding information. Nor did I enjoy keeping Ken Jackson in the dark; he's a good cop and I know he smelled a rat, though he was too loyal to say so.'

'There are pluses as well,' Hannah reminded him. 'You came to understand—and perhaps appreciate—your parents a bit better. And best of all, you're free of that longstanding fear that your father might have been involved in Dick's disappearance.'

'True, and Sheila's free of her ghosts. What's more, I think we can safely say the family feud's at an end. Larry Vernon rang with his congratulations, and the rift with Jenny has been healed.'

'Jenny?'

'Jenny Makepeace-that-was.' He grinned for the first time in two weeks. 'An old sweetheart of mine.'

'You dark horse! You never mentioned her before.'

'It was a Romeo and Juliet situation—young love torn apart by warring families. It was—good—to see her again, and straighten things out.'

'Should I be jealous?' Hannah asked lightly.

He shook his head, laying a hand over hers. 'No, my love. She was then and you are now. Still, it's good to be on speaking terms again. And I've a bit more news for you: Sheila's going to invite us to her annual garden party, along with the Vernons and the Makepeaces. How about that?'

He wondered how Colin and Rona would handle the situation. Quite well, he thought. They'd accepted the inevitable and in time their memories would mellow into nostalgia, as his and Jenny's had. But that was something he couldn't discuss with Hannah.

She'd been watching his face, aware there was still something he was holding back, but content that it should be so. 'All in all, it's been quite a case, hasn't it?' she commented.

'It has, and I'm certainly glad it's over.'

She pushed back her chair. 'And since supper's over too, let's go through for coffee.'

He followed her into the sitting-room and strolled over to the window. On the grass beneath, old Mrs Taverner was again replenishing the birds' water, and the sight of her battered straw hat gave him deep satisfaction. He'd watched her the night the case began; it was fitting she should appear again now it was ending.

Somehow, it helped to put things in perspective that, all

the time he'd been engaged in traumatic events—opening graves, gazing on skeletons—she had continued quietly ministering to the birds. Ordinary life went on, whatever world-shattering events were taking place, and there was comfort in that.

'Coffee's poured,' said Hannah's voice behind him, and, abandoning his fancies, he took his place beside her.